In The Darkness, Be The Light

Cathy Wood Newman

In The Darkness, Be The Light

www.bluebayoubreeze.com

This work contains pure fiction, any coincidences are precisely coincidence.

ISBN: **979-8-9858446-0-3**

DEDICATION

I give thanks and glory to God who continues to bless me with the ability to capture my imagination to share with y'all in my novels and devotionals.

Thank you to my husband, family and fans who pushed me to finish the second book in this series even when life took the wheel and turned down a ravine.

And to my editors Tara, Jerry & Elizabeth, y'all helped me keep the story flowing, thank you.

Table of Contents

CHAPTER ONE

Be Still and Let Your Light Shine

My eyes fluttered as I slowly sat up placing my palms on the damp mossy cement next to me. I gingerly cupped the back of my throbbing head. The gas lanterns in the courtyard began to flicker indicating it was about 6 p.m. A small yellow butterfly haphazardly fluttered around pausing on my shoulder for a moment before continuing up and over the tall green hedges.

I wondered, *What happened? How long have I been here?*

Repositioning my feet in my black shoes I steadied myself before standing. Dusting my hands on one another and then running them down my thin charcoal pencil skirt with a flicking motion, I watched as small particles swirled slowly to the brick paved ground.

Waiting for my mind to catch up to me I realized I missed Aunt Nina's interment! How could I have let that happen? Getting my footing I rushed toward the overgrown entrance of the courtyard. Skidding to a stop as my eye caught something dark off to the right. *My bag!* I scooped it up examining the contents, two out of the 3 books were missing. *Not this again!* Someone took Papa's and Aunt Nina's book and left the one I was creating. I growled in annoyance, flapping the cover over the bag, and closing the opening.

The books live, they change, and they reveal chapters that weren't there before. I have unlocked papa's book and read it numerous times. These books are more than just knowledge of spells and the history of each of their authors' lives. Aunt Nina's book remained locked because the unique item required to open it has not been uncovered yet. It had only been a few weeks since she unexpectedly passed away. She was my mentor and I felt lost not having her to guide me. I paused remembering when Charlie, Aunt Nina's nephew, and I found her on her front porch. She looked so peaceful in the swamp. Although she was not my Aunt, she had no children of her own and everyone called her Aunt Nina. Charlie introduced us and knew the deep spiritual bond we had. He gave me her book after she died.

I tossed the long strap over my left shoulder. Inhaling deeply, I let my mind process everything, I remembered I was supposed to meet Father Verum after the service. He didn't show up. I examined the area around the courtyard. There was a faint haze engulfing the perimeter. I carefully put my palms up to the haze without touching it. Holding my breath, I pressed through it. A rushing wind deafened my ears as the haze swirled into a whirlwind disappearing into the evening sky.

Standing with my palms still out in front of me, I rubbed my fingertips together thinking I will have to write all this down in my own book when I get home.

I hustled to the wrought iron gate and rattled it. Pressing my face between the bars of the locked gates I tried to peer down the street to locate help. The leafy palms around me swayed and I spun around. This was eerily similar to what happened right before I was knocked out. "Who is there?" I demanded. "Show yourself!"

The leaves parted and a wrinkled face appeared, "Miss, how did you get in here?" The man asked in confusion.

"I was meeting someone."

"I didn't see you before. How did you get in here?" He asked me again.

"Can you let me out?" I asked deflecting his question.

He shook his head and pulled out a large metal key ring searching for the one to unlock the gate. "You shouldn't be back here." He scolded me, holding the gate open for me to exit.

"Thank you." I said politely and rushed around to the front of The Saint Louis Cathedral. The man was right; everything was locked up. Looking around I was hopeful to see anyone I recognized, but Jackson Square was practically empty. Her service ended hours ago. Most people were eating supper before the night crowd took over.

I turned down St. Peter Street toward St. Louis Cemetery No. 1. After a brisk 10-minute walk there, I arrived to see those wrought iron

2

gates were locked too. The night air pushed a chill through me as the cold front arrived in New Orleans. Rubbing my arms to cut the coldness, I walked down St. Anne Street back toward Royal Street heading to my mom's house on the corner of Governor Nicholls Street.

Hopefully, Charlie was there. Surely, he did not go all the way to his home in the swamp tonight. My mind raced with questions I could not answer. I could not wait to pour them out of my mind and talk with Charlie. My toes were freezing so I picked up my pace. Desperate to get inside I told myself *Only about 6 more blocks to go.* The sun had now completely set and darkness filled the streets.

Encouraging myself to keep going I continually whispered to myself, "Arielle, you are almost home." The recurring annoying feeling crept in like the tickling on my forehead and the tightness in my chest. *What now?!?* I glanced around to see if anyone was following me. As the temperature seemed to drop a few degrees a shadow draped over me from above. Kicking my low heels off, I scooped them up, and began trotting barefoot down the uneven sidewalks desperate to reach the warmth and safety of home. Bam! Startled by the loud clap when a leather-bound book slammed to the ground, I stopped in my tracks.

Reaching for the open book on the sidewalk I wondered if it could that be Papa's book or Aunt Nina's? Just as my fingers touched the cover, it evaporated into a red mist.

Another trick, how could I be so dense? Breathe deeply, center yourself. Standing up I raised my gaze to meet what had forced me to stop. I felt my jaw open in disbelief, as I stretched my arm out. My fingers felt the cold mist from the white billowing cloak. "Aunt Nina, is that really you?" She was engulfed in a soft pink light. She smiled and her eyes danced. My eyes followed her outstretched arm to her pointing finger. A hand carved wooden sign hung from the shop with the words "The Egrets' Nest." Aunt Nina raised her cloak and floated toward the emerging stars

I cried out, "Wait! I don't know where your book is. I need you, don't leave me!"

Her voice whispered, "Be still, and let your light shine." The pink light popped and faded like a firework in the dark sky.

Standing in the darkness, blinking rapidly as reality set in, my toes and fingers were numb from the cold. I took off in a full run as much as my skirt would allow. Slamming into the front door, twisting the knob yanking the door open, I stumbled into the warm house. I hollered, "Charlie? Mama?" Rounding the foyer into the kitchen I ran smack into Mark, my older brother.

He grabbed my shoulders and lightly shook me causing my hair to fly in my face, "Where have you been, Arielle?" A deep wrinkle formed across his brow showing his concern.

Mama spun me around to cup my face, brushing the strands behind my ears, "We have been worried sick about you! You are freezing, let me get you a blanket."

"Where is Charlie?"

"He went home." Mama called out, as she dug for a blanket.

"I didn't make it to the cemetery, I wanted to talk to him. Was he upset?" I asked them.

"What happened to you?" Mark asked, standing with his arms crossed.

"Was Father Verum at the interment?" I asked, not answering Mark.

"Yes, of course he was there, he did the service. Why?" Mama said as she draped the heavy blanket over my shoulders guiding me to the couch to sit with me.

"What time did he get there?" I asked, still not answering any of their questions.

"Arielle what is this all about?" Mama asked firmly.

"I was attacked," I blurted out, then asked, "Was he late?"

"What do you mean you were attacked?" Her voice raised an octave sitting up straight as a board. "I am calling the police. Filing a report." She wagged her finger at me, "I did call to say you were missing, but they wouldn't do anything for 24 hours. And now look, you were attacked!"

"I'm fine now, just a little bump on my head." I said softly touching the sore spot.

"Did they steal your wallet? Where were you?" She reached for my bag that was still across me.

Pulling my bag back, "Mama, I am fine. I have my wallet." I said calmly to try to get her to slow down.

"Mark, how long are you staying?" *Maybe I could get him alone and ask him some questions* I thought.

"Nicole and Ethan are already at home. Now that I know you are safe, I'm going." He said pointing his thumb at the front door.

"Okay, I will call you later." I said making sideways eye contact blinking rapidly at him. He knew all the odd things going on in my life. Mama didn't and the less she knew the better. Mark kissed Mama on her forehead and headed out.

I rose from the couch and slowly placed the blanket next to her, "Mama, I'm going to go upstairs and call Charlie to see if he made it home safely."

She nodded and left the room quietly. I followed and watched from the doorway as she randomly wiped the countertop.

"Mama?" I asked gently.

"Yes?" She said in a whisper, making small circles with the damp cloth focused on her task.

"Look at me." I pleaded.

She glanced at my eyes glistening then back down at the cloth she now folded in half.

"I'm sorry." I said arms stretched out.

She slapped the dish towel down on the counter and she hugged me too tight.

"Mama, I'm sorry I worried you. I didn't do it on purpose!" I explained.

She pulled back as we locked eyes, "Arielle, you're still my little baby girl and this town isn't safe."

"I know Mama and I'm very careful, but things happen from time to time that I don't have any control over." I tried to explain.

She kissed my forehead and let me escape from her long embrace, "Go call Charlie."

"Good night, Mama, I love you."

"Good night, love you too."

The phone rang and rang, no answer. I took a long hot shower to take the rest of the chill out of my bones. Calling again still no answer. His answering machine must be full since it never picked up.

Be still and let your light shine. Thoughts of the Egret's Nest flooded my mind. I tried to call Charlie a few more times, but still no answer. I was trying not to worry, but he just lost his aunt, he had to be hurting and to make things worse I wasn't there for him. I fell asleep repeating Aunt Nina's words, *"Be still, let your light shine".*

The morning light drifted in my room diffused from the sheer curtains. I laid still, snuggled in the warm covers, *Thank you God for all you do for me. Help me find the books. Continue to heal Charlie in his*

6

grief. Help me to still figure out my true path. Protect my family. Guide me to find a new mentor since you took Aunt Nina from me. Oops, sorry. I didn't mean it like that, maybe a little. Wow this prayer really took a wrong turn. Okay, focus Arielle. Thank you and sorry. I know you are in control. Help me to be still and let my light shine. Whatever that exactly means. Amen.

Kicking my leg to move the covers I tested the air temperature with my foot, before pulling all the covers back. My foot retracted like a turtle back into its shell, waiting a few more minutes. Wrapping my fuzzy robe tightly around me, I shuffled down the hall to the bathroom. Sounds of the ringing house phone were muffled by the closed bathroom door. It only rang a few times. I hollered from the banister, "Mama? Did you get the phone?"

"Yes," she called back.

Padding down the stairs I met her in the kitchen. "Was it, Charlie?"

"Yes." She answered and continued to flip the last pancake on the stove.

"Well?! What did he say?"

"He asked for you to call him." She said plainly.

"That is, it?" I said with a little too much annoyance in my voice.

"Yes. I told him you made it home. He said to call him when you get a chance." She said putting the rest of the dirty dishes in the sink and asked, "Pancakes?"

"I need some coffee." I said in a low voice.

"Yes, you do, Ms. Grumpy." She said taking her cup upstairs to get ready for the day. Leaving the plate of pancakes for me to eat.

Stretching the wall phone cord across the kitchen to sit at the kitchen table with my steaming cup of coffee the phone rang and rang, still no answer. Maybe I am dialing the wrong number? Carefully punching in each number, I tried again. Still no answer and no answering machine, slamming the phone down on the receiver.

Aunt Nina's voice filled my head, "*Be still and let your light shine*". I rolled my eyes and headed upstairs leaving the pancakes.

CHAPTER TWO

The Egret's Nest

Cupping my mouth over the phone and talking softly so Mama couldn't hear me I said, "Mark, you're not going to believe what happened after the service."

"What did happen?" he asked.

"Well, I was supposed to meet Father Verum in the courtyard."

"Why?" He quizzed.

"He wanted to talk to me, but he didn't tell me why because the service was about to start."

"Oh. So, did you meet him?" he asked.

"No, he didn't show up." I said louder than I meant too.

"That isn't like Father, he keeps his word."

Sighing, "I know, but it gets weirder, and I wanna know if he was late?"

"I dunno Arielle, I wasn't really paying attention. I didn't notice him being really late. How did it get weirder?"

"Well, when I got to the courtyard Father was not there, but something in the bushes caught my eye and before I knew it someone knocked me out and stole Papa's and Aunt Nina's books."

"Did you call the police?" Mark asked.

"No."

"I think Mama is right, you should file a report." Mark advised.

"There's more to it." I explained.

"Okay." He said waiting for my reason to not call the police.

"When I woke up, I was in something like a bubble. Whoever took the books cast a spell around me making me invisible. The groundskeeper never saw me until I asked him to let me out of the locked gates. Then I went straight to the cemetery. But everyone was gone so I came home, and you know the rest."

"Why not call the police? Just leave out the bubble part so they don't think you are crazy." he continued to press.

"Why? What do I report? I don't know what happened. I got knocked out before I saw anyone." My annoyance was on the rise, "Are you going to help me or not?"

"Arielle, what do you want from me?"

"I want to know if Father Verum is behind this, of course!" Now I was starting to get really irritated.

"Why don't you just confront him and ask him if he took the books?" Mark suggested plainly.

"If he did, do you think he will be honest? I mean, if he is going to steal, why wouldn't he lie?"

"You are getting a little crazy about all of this. There's only one way to find out, ask him."

"Okay, thanks for nothing Mark." I said, pushing a long sigh out.

"Look, I'm sorry you got hurt, but I'm obviously not much help to you. Go see Father and let me know what he says. You're being a little ridiculous." Mark said.

"Whatever. I'll talk to you later." I said, rolling my eyes.

"Bye, l'il sis!" he said dripping with sarcastic sweetness.

Go right to the source. Maybe Mark was right, but I don't want to admit that to him quite yet. I bundled up to walk over to The Egret's Nest to poke around and get my thoughts together. During my slow stroll I worked up a plan. I could go to Charlie's camp in the swamp and take a day trip to visit Father Verum too.

A small brass bell jingled as I pushed the large door into the shop. It jingled a second time as the door closed. A thin older man with bright blonde wiry hair fluffed out under his black beret peeked around the corner. As he looked at me with one brow raised, his eyes were amplified by his thick glasses. The strong smell of cigarette smoke filled my nose as he drew closer. He wrung his hands, "Can I help you find something, dear?"

"Um no, I am just browsing. Thank you." I glanced around at the front room filled with a myriad of antique items from furniture to dishes.

I could hear the sound of his coarse hands rubbing together as he said, "Very well," Turning, he walked behind the large counter and stood behind the brass register.

I wandered around the shop with my arms folded; I didn't want to knock anything over then being forced to pay for it. Pausing, I looked at a watercolor of the swamp hanging on the wall. I blurred my focus on the picture and I saw the clerk's reflection watching me. His eyes narrowed, his hairs grew to long points, and his nose turned into a snout. I spun around to look at him, but he was looking down at the register.

"Yes?" He said, looking up slowly at me. His appearance was normal.

I swallowed hard and said, "Actually do you have any information on Egret's Nests?"

He shuffled down the narrow hallway and I followed him to the back of the shop. I gave a slight cough from the smell of musty old books filling my nostrils. He unclamped his hands to wave at a section of books in the corner of the room. Although the windowpane in the backdoor of the room was dusty it added a little extra light to the dim room.

"Great thanks, I'll check it out." I said turning sideways to squeeze around him in the tight hallway.

He nodded, wandering back to the front of the shop.

Each room in the back of the building was full of books. There was an entire bookshelf about egrets. I pulled off my quilted coat, placed it on the floor using it as padding to kneel on and started at the bottom section and worked my way up. The jingle of the bell came and went a few times. Although I did not know quite what I was looking for at this point, the muffled speech of the clerk and customers didn't distract me from my search. Okay is this pointless? Once again, I could use some help down here!

"Meow."

My hair flung to the left and to the right as I searched for the source of the sound. Nothing. With a slight eye roll of annoyance, I continued to thumb through each book looking for anything of importance or a sign.

"Meow."

"Kitty?" My eyes scanned the room as I moved my head slowly this time.

Flump, a book landed next to me with a cloud of dust dancing around it. I gazed up at the very top of the shelf. There sat an orange tabby cat with a bit of a smirk. "Hey, I know you! You are Aunt Nina's spirit guide. What are you doing here?" I cooed at him.

"Meow." He gracefully leapt off the top of the bookcase, disappearing into thin air, then reappearing as he landed on his front paws with his back ones meeting them. He pressed his face against my leg with a soft purr then flopped down on his side. I began to scratch behind his ear, but my hand passed through him showing me he was just an illusion.

The clerk tapped on the door frame, "I see you met our new resident. He showed up last night and just made himself at home. I named him Marmalade."

"He's a sweetie, nice to meet you, Marmalade." I said winking so only the cat could see me.

"You finding what you need in here? It's not a library you know." His tone changing to annoyed.

"I'm sure I'll find it when it strikes me, thanks for asking." I said turning back to the bookcase.

"Hum." he replied, watching until the jingle from the bell broke his creepy gaze and he went back up front.

"He thinks you are real, doesn't he?" I asked Marmalade. I slowly swiped my hand through this body and asked, "Why are you not fully here like when Aunt Nina was alive?"

The shelf of books began to radiate a rainbow of colors as if there was a prism bouncing with a sunbeam. The colors swirled around the room. I stood and spun around with my arms out dancing with the colors. Slowly the colors evaporated.

I picked up the book that Marmalade pushed to the floor to get my attention. It had a tiger on the cover, so I placed it back on the shelf. A book pulsed a soft plum color, I could see the color flow from the top and bottom of the spine near the pages. I tapped the book with my index finger once. Putting my nail in my mouth I waited a few seconds.

"You must be what I am looking for. Right Marmalade?" I asked not taking my eyes off the book as it jiggled, pulling out away from the others. I hooked the top of the book with my finger pulling it out. *How annoying was this!* I thought to myself seeing a small gold lock on it. The cover was embossed with a single feather. I flipped the book around looking for a barcode or a price. There was a small red sticker with a hand printed $27. Wow, he must be proud of this book at that price, but I need it for some reason.

"Thanks Marmalade." I attempted to give him a little scratch under his chin, but still couldn't feel him. Then I started for the door. Marmalade jumped in front of me causing me to stumble. "What's that for?" I asked him.

He let out a low growl and puffed up, not letting me leave the room.

"Okay, Okay." I said with my hand up like I was about to be arrested, with the one book still in my hand. I sat down on the floor placing the book and my jacket next to me. "Come here, it's okay."

He came and curled up in my lap and we just sat together. Another jingle from the door sounded. We sat quietly. I could hear a man talking to the clerk. It was a familiar tone although muffled. I started to get up and move closer to the door. Marmalade again let out a low growl. Crawling to sit inside the door I tilted my head to hear what they were saying to each other. *Who is that? I know that voice,* I tried to recognize it.

"Yes, I am very interested in your new find. When would you like to meet?"

"Tonight. Right after closing time." He replied to the clerk.

"Our usual place?" The clerk asked.

"Yes." The bell jingled as the familiar voice left.

"Hey! Are you ever going to buy anything or not?" The clerk hollered.

"Yes sir, I found my treasure!" I called back scrambling off the floor. Marmalade evaporated before I could thank him.

The clerk gave me a side glance as he typed in the amount into the cash register, "You know there isn't a key for this book, right?" He

14

asked, "No returns either. Don't go trying to open it and break it and expect to give it back to me." He glared at me.

"I take it you have experienced this before?" I tried to joke with him.

He huffed. "Your total is $28.09."

I reached in my purse and gave him a ten- and twenty-dollar bill.

I had the new book securely in my bag along with the book I was creating. I had written all the details of each of my encounters, battles, and even small happenings. I found a bench under an oak tree to record what happened today at The Egret's Nest. Once everything was written onto the pages, I gazed around watching people and squirrels moving around the park.

I pulled out the new book and examined every inch turning it over searching for clues. I traced my index finger of the stitched binding on the book. A shadow flickered above my view and moved to the trees watching the sunlight flicker through the slightly bare branches. A falling leaf caught my sight and I watched it gently fall toward my face. The soft landing on my forehead revealed it was not a leaf, but a grey feather. Plucking the feather, I held it over the cover of my new book. The feathers didn't match in size, but the all over shape was the same. Just for fun I used the vein to try to pick the lock open.

The book gave a pulsing jolt through my hands. I dropped the book, released the feather, and said to the book, "Okay I see it isn't a fit." The book bounced once on the bench next to me. Glancing around I watched a gray squirrel scurry up the nearby oak tree. He perched on a branch and chewed on a nut he found. Picking up the feather I gently laid it on the cover of the book. The book bounced around on the bench shaking as the feather began to glow and was consumed by the embossed feather on the cover. "Did you just eat that feather?" I asked for the book quietly.

The book let out a loud burp as the corner of the pages rippled up some releasing air from inside.

I drew back from it saying, "Excuse you."

It hopped once more and settled down.

Speaking to the book again, "I could go for some lunch. Are you going to behave if I pick you up?"

It remained still and allowed me to place it back into my bag. We headed home so I could make a sandwich.

Along the way I picked up a few other feathers and tossed them into my bag feeding my new book. It continued to consume them and let out a belch each time. *What a gross book,* I thought to myself.

CHAPTER THREE

Answer the Phone

I could hear the deep ring of the kitchen phone through our front door. I struggled to get the key in the door and open in time. The answering machine picked up and I could hear Charlie's distant voice. Finally, the door was open, and I darted to catch him before he hung up. "Charlie? Charlie?" Silence. Ugh. I quickly called him back. The phone rang with no way to leave a message. I tried three more times. Mashing the red button on the answering machine.

Charlie's voice played "Hey Arielle not sure why you are not calling me and why you didn't come to Aunt Nina's service. Call me back, we need to talk." My stomach dropped and growled at the same time.

I paced the kitchen waiting for the grilled cheese sandwich to finish melting on the stove. I called Charlie again, no answer. Wiping the delicious grease from the corners of my mouth, I called Charlie one last time. Still no answer. This was becoming very strange. I decided I will go to his camp tomorrow.

For now, I needed to get prepared for a conversation with Father Verum about getting my books back. Remembering the things Aunt Nina had taught me, I placed a small bag of red clay that had been blessed to help ward off demons that might attack I double checked that my necklace was securely around my neck and slipped on the protective vest Aunt Nina made for me.

I can't believe she's gone. Because I'm still learning how to use my powers I have so many questions to ask her. Now that she's gone, who do I trust? I don't feel like I can trust Father Verum. Can I trust Father Beau? "Aunt Nina, are you there? Can you hear me?" I spoke softly. "I could use a little direction, please."

The ticking of the grandfather clock in the other room was the only sound in the house. Not even the familiar pitter patter of feet or a random giggle from a child ghost in the attic. It was still and quiet. Repeating what Aunt Nina's spirit told me: *Be still and let your light shine*. I knew what "be still" meant but what was the meaning of 'let your light shine'. The creak of the front door broke my train of thought. "Mama? Is that you?"

"Hey sweetie, did you eat dinner yet? I have some leftovers from Gallagher's. It's one of your favorites, soft shell crab in alfredo."

"I just finished a grilled cheese sandwich, but thanks Mama. I was about to head out."

"Where are you going, Charlie isn't in town, is he?"

"Oh, um, no he isn't, but Dixie wanted to get together and hang out a bit."

"That's nice, she seems to be spending all her time with her boyfriend. Making time for friends is important too," she reminded me, tapping me once on my nose.

"Yes, that's why we are doing a girls night. I may stay over at her house too." The lie just started to flow. My quickly developing plan was to approach the bookstore clerk. I needed to see what he was up to.

"Did you ever file that police report?" She asked.

"No, I didn't." I said, shaking my head.

"I really wish you would," she said, then raising her hand, cutting me off, "Even if you don't have a description of the person, they should make a record of it."

"I know," I said without making eye contact.

She gently grabbed my chin and looked at me, "Promise me you will?"

Unable to lie directly to her face I blinked long, "Yes Mama I will." I knew I would have to do it now.

"Thank you. Have a good time with Dixie. Love you," she said with a kiss on my forehead good night and started to walk toward the staircase.

"Love you too, Mama."

Pausing at the bottom of the stains she turned and looked at me, "Wait, don't you need an overnight bag?"

"I'll stop by and pick it up later." Trying to cover my poor lie.

Her hand fluttered toward me as if to say, do whatever you want and turned to go up the stairs.

Outside leaning on the front door wondering, *Did Mama buy it?* I gathered my courage and walked toward the Egret's Nest looking for somewhere to watch for Father Verum. Entering The Napoleon House restaurant, I sat down at one of the tables near the French doors which gave me a perfect view of the Egret's Nest. Still hungry and needing a reason to be allowed to sit in the restaurant, I placed an order, which quickly arrived. Joyfully I spooned the warm caramel bread pudding for my first bite. The sweet dessert complimented the warm black coffee with a touch of creamer.

Trying to divide my attention between the dessert and watching for the clerk was difficult. My dessert called to me wanting my full attention! I peered over my warm cup of coffee at the shop between bites. A tall man in a long dark coat tapped on the door of the Egret's Nest but did not go inside. He continued walking up Chartres Street away from Jackson Square.

I waved frantically at the waitress. Catching her sight, I pointed to the cash I placed on the table. I sighed looking at my half-eaten dessert thinking *I am sorry to leave you behind.*

Glancing back at the shop, I saw the clerk emerge. He quickly locked the door walked in the same direction as the other man. Pacing myself I continued down Chartres Street and watched them turn on St Louis Street and then on Dauphine Street. The man disappeared into an old building with the clerk following close behind.

I glanced around seeing the street was empty I crossed to the building the men entered. I placed my hands on the cold moss-covered brick windowsill, peeking in the windows. The thick dust on the windows made it impossible to see anything. I rubbed a circle with the sleeve of my jacket to no avail. I shivered as the temperature dropped. My heart skipped a beat when the dark windows suddenly lit up with a bright flash of red. I wondered *What was going on? Only one way to find out, you must go inside.*

I slowly opened the door and quietly stepped inside, pulling the door closed. Once again, the hallway lit up with the red flash. The sounds of men arguing floated down the hallway. I moved towards the wall as I looked around the room, noticing the furniture was covered by white drop cloths. As I crept down the hallway to the first room, my slow steps were undetected by the men in the other room. The door was closed. I paused to listen for their distant voices traveling down the hall. I continued toward the next room. There it was again. Another red flash. This time it came from under the closed door on my left.

"Try it again!" the man commanded.

"I already did, this isn't working. This was a waste of my time," said the clerk.

"I told you I have the books, but you have to bring something to open them."

"I'm not buying another useless locked book from you again. I have a shop full of them now," the clerk pointed out.

"They are not useless! They contain more power than you've ever imagined. We just have to get them open, and you'll see," the man fussed at the clerk. "We need her to open them" he stressed.

20

"I'm leaving," the clerk quipped. "We can make a deal when you open the books."

I scrambled to get back in the front room to hide. The old wooden floor creaked giving away my position.

"What's that noise? Did you hear that? Someone's in here," the clerk said as he came out of the room. I had just curled up under a white draped cloth. Breathing shallowly, I waited.

"You are paranoid; no one's here," the man muttered. "Come back and let's try again."

"No, I'm done with these games. When you figure out how to open these books, you can meet me for a price."

"You're not going anywhere," he said, getting a little louder with each word. The room filled with a red hazy light.

I peeked around out of my hiding place to see what was going on. The clerk was hunched on the ground with Father Verum standing over him, arms outstretched. The clerk groaned, "Okay, stop!"

"I thought you'd come around. Now get up and get back in there."

Realizing that the man was Father Verum I gasped. I quickly cupped my mouth to try to hide any more noise. My eyes widened watching the transformation of the clerk. He shook his head like a wet dog as his ears popped out and grew long. His nose elongated into a snout, and he wiggled it in my direction. "She's in here."

"Who?" Father asked.

"The girl from the shop today," the clerk growled.

The dust from the sheet got the best of me and I squeaked out three short sneezes. There was no more hiding, pulling back the sheet I stood for Father and the clerk to see me.

"Arielle, what in the world are you doing here?"

"I was going to ask you the same thing, Father."

"You should scoot along." He commanded, waving his hand at me with a concerned but stern voice.

"I'm not going anywhere till you return the books you took from me. They were not yours." He raised his hand and walked slowly toward me, "I assure you I don't know what you're talking about."

"You're the only one that knew we were meeting in the back of the church. Give me my books," I said with my hand outstretched from across the room.

"I don't have them."

"Lies again," I said standing firm, "Give the books to me now!" Stamping my left foot.

"Come now; you should be leaving." Father motioned for me to come toward him with a sly smile as he moved closer.

Still in the form of a wolf standing upright with hair puffed out under his clothes, the clerk said, "We don't want any trouble."

"Really Mr. Wolf? You look like trouble to me," I said, backing away from Father.

He glanced down realizing his form, shaking as if to dry himself from water, he transformed back into the wiry hair clerk from today. "Better? See no trouble here." He extended his arms as if just doing a normal illusion or card trick.

I took a step toward the front door. "My brother's outside waiting for me, so you better just let me go."

"We are not holding you hostage. Go," Father said dismissively, trying to shoo me away.

The clerk whispered to Father, "She has seen too much, you can't just let her go."

22

Father placed his hand on the clerk's arm to hush him looking me in the eyes, "No. She's leaving."

"You don't know what I am capable of doing to you Mr. Wolf," I said as I took a few more steps toward the door realizing that Father was trying to get me out of here safely. "This isn't over, you know. I will get my books back and use them against you."

My purse began to levitate between us, the flap opened as my new purchase floated out. The embossed egret feather popped off the cover and fed itself into the lock on the front. With a quick twist the book was open. It began flopping on the floor as dozens of feathers flew out. Pages frantically turned, stopping in the middle of the book. A brilliant yellow beam of light touched the ceiling. An image of a woman appeared in the light.

Mr. Wolf gasped, "Madame Fia!"

Father stepped back pushing the clerk in front of him for protection. I ducked behind another covered piece of furniture to protect myself.

"Who disturbs my eternal rest?" Madame Fia hissed, spinning around scanning the room. Her gaze landed on the clerk.

He stuttered, "Not me Madame, it was her!" Pointing directly at the chair I was hiding behind.

I slowly rose knowing there was no way I could escape through the front door at this point.

"What do you want, girl?" The glowing figure changed from a yellow glow to a dark orange color.

"I'm sorry. I don't quite know how it all happened. What do I want?" repeating her question. Pointing back at the two men, "I would like to get away from these two and get back my books that Father stole from me."

She spun with her long dread locks flowing around her, facing Mr. Wolf and Father Verum. "What do you want from me? Why am I being called from my eternal rest?"

Father leaned around Mr. Wolf, "Possibly you are here to assist us?" he suggested.

"I highly doubt that. I'm not your servant." she retorted. "What year is this?"

"It's 1985," Mr. Wolf answered.

"I don't want to be here," Madame Fia said with anger as she started to levitate higher in the room.

"We don't want any trouble, you could just return to your book, couldn't you?" I asked.

"How do you presume I do that when I didn't come out on my own accord?" Madame Fia responded with agitation.

Taking slow steps toward the front door I uttered, "I think you should take it up with those two and I will just head out."

A bolt of orange shot out toward the door igniting it on fire. Flames billowed toward the ceiling. I immediately pulled away from the crackling flames moving toward Mr. Wolf and Father. I looked toward the men with questioning eyes.

Father said to me, "Why don't you do something? You are the one with the strongest powers." Fluttering his hand toward Madame Fia.

"Perhaps you called me for a battle to build your strength? You think you can steal my powers? Just try, little girl." With a slight bow and her red dress flowing around her Madame Fia invited me toward her.

"I don't think that's such a good idea." Grimacing and showing my bottom teeth.

"Do you have a better idea?" Mr. Wolf asked.

"Why don't you attack her Mr. Wolf?" I suggested.

"Enough!" Madame Fia yelled. Extending her arms two streams of fire shot from her palms and engulfed the room. We escaped the hall into a back room.

"Now what?" I asked.

"You have to go out there and extinguish her." Father commanded me.

"Excuse me, but like hell I do. Why don't we just go out the back door?" I suggested.

"The back door is a portal to another dimension; you really don't want to go that way." Mr. Wolf warned me.

"Fantastic. Really guys, could you have picked any better place to meet?" I said dripping with sarcasm. I continued, "I don't know what to do with her. I don't even know anything about her."

"I will tell you all her history after you defeat her," Mr. Wolf said, "Actually, you can just read her book when you are done," he chuckled a little.

"That is not helpful." I jumped when a bolt of fire flew by the doorway, "Okay y'all owe me and you better give me my book back after all of this." Swirling my arms in alternate circles I formed a teal blue bubble of protection and peeked down the hallway.

A line of fire smacked into my bubble dissolving into a mist. I ducked back into the room satisfied we were at least protected. Next, I needed to conjure water to put out that fire! Until now I had only created lightning bolts. Thinking of the old game, rock, paper, scissors concept, you can't beat fire with fire, so to speak. Water, who can I call on to help me with water? Aunt Nina? She lived on the water.

"Aunt Nina I could use a little help. If you can fill me with water, that would be awesome," I whispered.

I looked down the hallway only to be attacked with a stream of fire bolts again. Placing my wrist together and opening my palms I let out a jolt of lighting. My blue light and her orange fire illuminated the room even more.

Father called out, "That isn't helping. Use water."

"I would if I knew how!" I shouted back at him.

Father chanted from the room as Madame Fia shot more and more fire at my bubble. Luckily, each round dissolved again into a mist.

He called to me, "Try again." Then he continued to chant.

Again, I assumed my stance, a tiny stream of water fluttered out of my palms making a small puddle of water on the floor. Madame Fia chuckled at me and spat fire down on my protective bubble creating a mist. It became so dense we were now in a fog with fire. I could hear Mr. Wolf and Father now chanting together.

"Again!" Father yelled at me.

My poor protection bubble began to fade as the fire engulfed the hallway, making its way down to the room we were in. I shot again. This time a steady stream about the thickness of a hose poured out extinguishing some of the flames around me.

Stepping into the hallway I cried out, "Keep chanting. I think it is helping."

As The smoke filled the house, I could hear the men coughing. Making two bubbles, I gently pushed them down the hallway to help the men stay safe. Fixing my dissolving bubble as best I could I turned back toward Madame Fia trying again. This time a firehose spray came from me pushing me back against the wall with such force it knocked the wind out of me. This caused a new part of my bubble to fracture, allowing smoke to creep into my space. I stopped to patch the fracture again. Aunt Nina's voice came to me again. *Be still and let your light shine.* I stood firm with fire filling the room, breathing deeply, arms outstretched with palms up.

26

"Madame, I am the light; return to the darkness from which you came" I commanded her.

The room froze in time. I stepped out of my bubble into the still flames. I ran my fingertips over them without any harm while walking over to Madame Fia. I knelt, taking the book in my hands, slamming it shut and causing the feather to re-emboss itself onto the cover. Everything in the room including Madame and the black smoke was sucked back into the book and the lock clicked shut. The smoke, fire, and even the water was completely gone. I put the book back in my purse.

Walking down the hall into the room where the two men were frozen in their bubbles in mid-chant, I took the moment to slowly search the room. There was a velvet bag with some odd items, and a few other books I didn't recognize. Maybe Father was telling the truth about my books.

I would deal with them later. Walking to the front door and out of the building I reached just my right hand back inside the door and snapped my fingers once releasing them back into current time. Taking a deep breath, I ran all the way home. My mind is filled with questions. *If Father doesn't have my books, then who does, Mr. Wolf? If Father was protecting me, why was he with Mr. Wolf?*

CHAPTER FOUR

A Safe Haven

Back home I climbed the stairs to find Mama waiting for me at the top landing.

"Arielle, were you at a bonfire tonight?"

"No, why?" I asked without making eye contact as I continued to climb the stairs.

"You smell like burnt wood."

Passing by her quickly, I said, "Oh yeah, um, all the more reason for me to shower. Right?"

"I guess you had a good time with Dixie tonight?" she called after me as I rounded the door frame into my room.

"Yes, Mama I did." I hated lying to her, but I had been able to keep Mama out of all the mess of my life and wanted to keep it that way for as long as possible.

"Arielle?"

I peeked my head out of the door, "Yes?"

"Is everything okay?"

"Of course, why do you ask?"

"I was talking to Ms. DeeDee, and she mentioned that Dixie and Ernie were out on a date tonight."

"Oh." I was totally caught in my lie.

"I am going to ask you again, Arielle, is everything okay?" She crossed her arms and gave me a stern look with her eyes.

"Yes Mama, I am fine."

"If you weren't with Dixie, where were you?"

"I was just out."

"Who were you with?"

I paused trying to decide what route to take.

Mama continued, "Look Arielle, I know you are thinking you are an adult, but if you are living in my house you need to follow my rules. Do you understand? We don't lie," she said, moving closer to me.

"Yes, Mama," I replied looking down to pick at my chipped nail polish.

"You have never been a troublemaker, why now?" She pleaded for an answer.

"I dunno, Mama. I'm not doing anything bad; I promise."

"Then why are you lying about who you are hanging out with? I just don't understand. I expect this kind of behavior from Mark, but not you!"

"I'm doing some research you could say."

"You are not taking any classes, what kind of research are you talking about?" she probed.

"Well, I want to know more about the book Papa left for me and it has brought up some questions."

"Okay, now we are moving in a positive direction." She smiled a little. Reaching for my hands trying to draw me into eye contact with her, she caringly said "Arielle, I want you to open up to me. I want to know what is going on in your life."

"Okay Mama, I'll try. I was just trying to figure some things out on my own," I said, locking eyes with her to show her I was being honest.

"I can relate to that; I was a young adult too." She looked off with a dreamy look in her eyes.

"I'm sorry Mama; I will do better."

"Do you want help with the research? I can help you; we can go to the library together."

"No, I want to do this on my own, like a little quest of sorts." I smiled at her.

"Okay I'll let you be. Just be honest with me. I am your Mama, and I will always find out if you are lying!"

"I will, good night, Mama."

"Good night sweetie." She paused and turned back toward me, "You know your Papa was working on that book right before he passed away. I never read it because he said it was just for you, but I know he was writing in it even before you were born."

I stepped out into the hallway and leaned against the wall next to my room, "So he was writing the book for me before I was born?" I asked.

"He had that book when we were dating. I asked him to share it with me, but every time he did the pages were blank."

"Blank?" I looked at her to see her facial expression.

"I accused him of erasing everything and not wanting to share. We had a pretty big blow up about it."

"I don't understand why some of the pages were blank." I admitted to her.

"I really didn't understand the whole thing either, but he tried to explain. There is more in this world than I can see. Something about the pages will appear when people need them the most."

"I can see his writing in his book, but there are sections that are blank."

30

"All the more reason that book was written for you. I don't even pretend to understand half the things your Papa was involved in, but I worry about your safety."

"Mama, I'm careful, I promise." I turned to head back into my bedroom.

"One more thing," Mama said, causing me to stop and turn back around. "Your Papa was working on something he said would be big right before he died. He was documenting it in his book."

"What was it?" I asked, stepping closer to her.

"He didn't explain it." She closed her eyes and took a deep breath. "But I think... I mean, I know he was sick, but... He might have been killed for what he was working on." Our eyes locked in the dim hallway.

"Mama, are you sure you don't know anything else?"

"He was very private about something, and I just didn't press him." She came closer and took my hand in hers, "Please be careful I cannot bear to lose anyone else."

"I will Mama," I said, squeezing her hand and nodding to assure her.

"You keep his book safe. It was very important to him," she told me with a hug.

I didn't have the heart to tell her I lost it along with Aunt Nina's. "Yes Mama."

I prayed that night for a good sleep and rest. Thankfully, I was granted it. The next morning, I decided to go visit Charlie, because I couldn't reach him by phone again. It would be nice to see him and tell him about my latest adventure. Normally, I would talk to his Aunt Nina, but since she passed, I don't have a new mentor to confide in. I really didn't know who to trust.

I started my day with a strong cup of coffee to get the energy and the inner warmth to face the cold trip.

"Mama, I'm heading out to visit Charlie."

"I'm sure he will be happy to have you for a visit." Her tone changed as she reminded me to behave.

"Yes, Mama I will. Love you," I replied as I swung my backpack over my shoulder and bounced out of the front door.

"Love you too, sweetie. Call me when you get there. Oh, and here take these pralines to Charlie."

I made the short motorcycle ride to our camp on the water. Nibbling on one of the pralines I watched the drab swamp. It was quiet and cold on the water. A few birds called in the distance, the water remained silent and calm. From there I navigated our small pirogue to Alligator Bend where Charlie lived. Our winters in southern Louisiana could get bone chilling cold with the added humidity. It had snowed a few times in my life, thankfully today wasn't one of those days. I had a heavy down jacket and thick gloves making it hard to hold onto the wooden oars. The trees were bare on the water, and the wildlife was scarce as I made my way through the curvy waterways.

I finally was getting the knack of navigating to and from our camps. My first trip I had my spirit animal Breeze, a white fluffy dog, guiding me. Today I was going solo. As I approached the bend, I saw the pier where I accidently fell and pulled Charlie in the water with me. The edges of my lips turned up reliving the amusing memory. He made a simple living here running an alligator farm and giving tours to kids to teach them about the life cycle of an alligator. Most of his business came from yearly scheduled school field trips.

I tied the boat to the pier and carefully disembarked. "Charlie?" I called from the pier. No answer. Climbing the stairs, I hollered again, "Charlie, are you here?" Tapping on the front door, "Charlie?" The door was unlocked, but I don't think he ever locked it anyway. Most people don't just show up to camps out in the swamp. Even though it was also a business for alligator tours, it was difficult to locate, and he usually picked up the tours and brought them to his farm. Jutting just my head inside the door I peeked in, "Charlie? Hello?" No answer.

I went inside and noticed in the small kitchen there was still a pot of hot coffee. Making myself at home I poured a cup. Searching inside his small camp, he wasn't inside. Walking the grounds with my coffee to help keep my hands warm, I walked the tour that Charlie gave me last year to see if he was tending to any of the alligator habitats. He wasn't anywhere to be found. *Maybe he was at his cousin's place not too far away?* I thought. I wasn't sure how to navigate there, so I waited.

I called Mama from Charlie's house phone, "Hi Mama, just wanted to let you know I'm at Charlie's."

"Good I am glad you finally got to talk to him."

"Well, not exactly. I can't find him. I plan on just staying a few days."

"You can't find him?" she said, alarmed.

"No, he isn't at his place, but by the looks of it he was here."

"Do you need me to come out there or send Mark?"

"No," I said, glancing out the window counting his airboats.

"Please be careful and call me once you find him. Maybe you could go to his cousin Nick's?"

Distracted, I muttered, "I guess I could try that."

"Are you sure you're, okay?"

"Yes. I think one of his boats is gone. He must have stepped out."

"Call me once you find him," she said sternly.

"I will. I promise," I said before I hung up.

I sat and waited. The sun was starting to set. I cleaned the coffee pot and my cup. I found a few snacks to nibble on before I found the comfort of the spare bedroom to sleep. The next morning Charlie still wasn't home. I was starting to worry.

"Okay spirits, can you give me a little guidance?" Sitting at the kitchen table with a fresh cup of coffee the tabby, Marmalade, appeared sitting on the table, but this time he was real as day.

Leaning back in my chair I said to him, "Fancy seeing you here. You plan on giving me some bad advice again like that book?" He glared at me and pushed my coffee cup on the floor and jumped off the table disappearing. "You little turd!"

Bending down to pick up the pieces of white ceramic, the coffee spill took shape. Moving and swirling creating a picture of monotone brown colors. It was Aunt Nina's camp with someone sitting on the porch. Charlie, he was at her camp! Tossing the coffee cup shards in the trash can, I quickly dabbed up the coffee scenery of Aunt Nina's camp. Grabbing my coat, gloves, and bag I hustled down the stairs to my little pirogue.

Paddling fiercely my arms began to burn from the constant motion. Bumping hard into the pier, I tied up next to one of Charlie's boats. "Charlie?"

I ran up the stairs taking them two at a time, "Charlie?" I grabbed the door swinging it wide and I ran smack into Charlie's square chest.

"Hey, slow down," he said, wrapping his arms around me.

I rested my head on his chest and sighed. Just feeling his warmth made me feel safe. Leaning back to look at his face, I gave him a soft slap on his cheek.

"What was that for?" He smirked, not letting me go.

34

"That is for not answering when I called, and for your answering machine not being turned on, and for leaving your coffee pot on making me drink old coffee," I rambled.

"Oh crap, I left the coffee pot on? I guess I have been a little scattered since Aunt Nina passed away."

"I forgive you." I said leaning back but still allowing him to wrap his arms around my waist. I continued, "I was worried about you."

"You were worried, what do you think I was when you didn't show up at the grave site?" My heart sank remembering we had not talked since I missed Aunt Nina's burial.

"Why didn't you wait to come back to the camp if you were so worried?" I asked defensively and pulled away from the embrace.

"I really just wanted to come home. I thought maybe it was too much for you and that is why you didn't come," he remarked, lowering his voice and his head.

"No, it's not like that, I promise. You have no idea what has been going on. Someone stole Papa's and Aunt Nina's books. I really need to get them back." I reached out and placed my hand on his arms. "I'm sorry I wasn't there for you."

He nodded, placing his hand over mine, and continued looking at the floor when he asked, "Were you able to get her book open?"

"No." I sighed.

"I mean I guess that is good it isn't open, right?" He was trying to find a silver lining in the situation.

"I feel so bad that it's gone!" I wailed. I proceeded to tell him about the Egret's Nest, the clerk aka Mr. Wolf, Father Verum, and Madame Fia. He listened quietly as I animatedly reenacted the encounter with Madame Fia. Once finished, I took a deep breath and waited for his response.

"Wow, I have so many questions," he said, "Like, what's up with Madame Fia, what is her problem? Why was Father with Mr. Wolf in the first place? And if Father was protecting you, do you think he really took the books?"

"Those are all things I have been rolling over in my mind too," I admitted.

With an understanding nod Charlie said, "I am glad you started here. I missed having you near." He held me in a loving embrace.

"I missed you too. How long are you staying here?" I inquired.

"Oh, I don't know. I was going through her things trying to decide what to do with the place and her stuff. Maybe there is something to help you unlock the book?" He suggested.

"Good idea. Hey, I'm going to call Mama and let her know I found you. She has been worried too."

"You will have to wait until we get back to my camp, Aunt Nina never did have a phone."

"Oh crap, I forgot."

Charlie took my hands in his, "I am glad you came all this way to see me."

"I wanted to make sure you knew I didn't just *not* show up. You are always there for me, Charlie. I want to be there for you."

He paused cupping my chin and tilting it, so our eyes met. "I am not mad at you."

My eyes blurred from the tears forming. "I know, but I feel awful not being there."

"Come here." He wrapped me in his warm arms again.

I let the tears flow, wetting his shirt. "I'm sorry."

"Okay that's enough, we can move past this," he said firmly.

"Okay." I nodded in agreement but sniffling a little.

"There has to be a clue that Aunt Nina left for you around here. Let's get to work."

I patted under my eyes, drying the rest of the tears away and nodded.

CHAPTER FIVE
Aunt Nina's Book

I took my time searching the house looking for clues to open her book. I could use the information in it to help me with my journey to learn more about my gifts. She was planning on teaching me more over the summer. Picking up random items I turned them over in my hands, examining them and placing them back. Nothing was speaking to me.

Charlie interrupted my wandering. "Do you want to sleep in Aunt Nina's room? I will take the guest room." He leaned against the door frame with his hair brushed to the left side of his face. His bronzed arms crossed over his faded T-shirt.

"Okay sounds good... Unless you want to share the guest room?" I suggested with a lift of a single eyebrow while walking slowly across the room to meet him in the doorway. The mood quickly changed as I banged my knee into the corner of the footboard. Clasping both palms over the injury I glanced up with a squished eyed smile.

"Arielle, I don't think that is a good idea. I don't want your papa visiting me from the dead in the middle of the night" he joked pointing at my tender knee. "I bet he's even responsible for that!"

I chuckled at the thought of it and gently patted my knee to diminish the lingering sting. *I would not put it past Papa to figure out a way to do that.*

"Can we spend tomorrow looking for clues again," I asked?

"Sounds like a plan. Good night." He moved from where he was leaning to place both hands on my arms above my elbows and gave me a short soft kiss on the lips. Then tapped the bottom of my chin with his index finger.

A little jolt of blue light escaped from my fingertips. "Good night, Charlie." I smiled and waved away the little fireworks, so he didn't see them.

Curling up in Aunt Nina's bed I pulled the covers to my chin and tossed and turned most of the night. Finally sleep took over and the room filled with a soft pink color. My eyes popped open, and I sat up in bed. A figure was perched at the foot of the bed. "Aunt Nina?" I whispered.

The figure turned and I could see her round face smiling. Marmalade was lounging in Aunt Nina's lap enjoying being petted from neck to tail. He hopped onto the bed and strolled toward me and began rubbing up against my arm and purring. My eyes flooded with a scene from the Egret's Nest. Mr. Wolf was tying up a man and shoving him in a closet. He worked quickly casting spells round the shop. The illusion of Marmalade appeared as Mr. Wolf said to him. "Do your work. Convince her to take this book." Shaking Madame Fia's book at him, "I need it open for my own survival."

My eyes returned to the pink room, and I asked the cat, "What are you saying?"

Aunt Nina spoke, "Marmalade was an illusion to trick you, he wasn't really there."

"But why?" I asked.

"Mr. Wolf is bad news. He is trying to use you to share the contents of Madame Fia's book with him. No matter what, you do not give him anything." The room faded into darkness, and they disappeared. I flopped back into the bed and drifted back to sleep.

The next morning, I woke to the smell of coffee and bacon. I really missed being with Charlie. Not only because I like him, but he is an exceptional cook. "What do we have this morning, chef?"

"Wow, you must have slept well," he joked.

I patted my hair trying to tame it, "Better?"

He laughed, "Excellent. Please sit, we have waffles, bacon, and coffee in honor of Aunt Nina."

"I'll toast to that," I said, raising my coffee mug!

"I didn't make any toast," Charlie joked again.

"I missed you, Charlie. Can we just stay in the swamp forever away from all the craziness?" It rolled off my tongue so quickly as I clapped my hand over my mouth, but it was too late, I had shared it out loud.

"Well, I can because I live here, but you have a destiny to fulfill, and I don't think it entails you hiding in the swamp."

"Maybe." My voice muffled by a mouthful of waffles and syrup. *Did he miss me?* I wondered if he just glossed over that part.

After cleaning up I sat on Aunt Nina's bed closing my eyes centering myself. *Okay, I need to find some answers. One, where are the books? Two, when I get the books, how do I open Aunt Nina's? Three, what do I do about Mr. Wolf and Father? Please feel free to answer any of them in any order!*

My eyes fluttered open to see a beautiful white egret on the porch railing. "Hello," I whispered to her. She cocked her head to look at me closer. "What are you doing here?"

She spread her wings wide and held the pose for several seconds. Turning her back to me, she took flight, gliding down to the pirogue. Again, she perched looking at me. I stood and leaned on the railing, waiting to see if she would just take off again. After a 5-minute stare off. I grabbed my coat and gloves heading down to her.

"Are you my spirit guide for the day," I asked her cheerfully?

Climbing into the back of the pirogue, I dipped the oars and pushed the boat out into the swamp. "Here we go."

The egret took flight and glided to stop in a nearby cypress tree. I followed down the small waterways as this continued for about an

40

hour. I had no idea where we were, and I realized I didn't even tell Charlie I was leaving. The sun was shining bright, keeping some of the chill out of the air. Once I caught up to her, the egret finally perched and stayed. Gracefully, she landed in my boat bow causing the boat to rock a little. "Now what?" I asked her.

She bolted straight up into the sky, disappearing.

"Hello?" My voice echoed off the still water.

Scanning the clear sky for the egret I noticed a small hole appear in the single cloud. A beam of light cast down on a tree, so I paddled over to the guiding light. Little peeping sounds were calling from the tree. Standing in the boat I steadied myself so I could tie the boat to a nearby cypress knee. Grabbing a low branch, I started to climb the thin branches up the tree keeping my foot close to the trunk for extra support. The more I climbed the louder the peeping of the birds got. As I approached the nest, I glanced around for the mama egret. Seven fuzzy white-grey birds popped out of the nest. All mouths were open eagerly waiting their next meal. An egret's nest, *what am I supposed to get from the nest? Surely not a baby bird!?* Watching the babies requesting food with each chirp there was a flash of rainbow colors in the nest. I gently reached in the nest dodging the sharp pain of baby beaks pecking on my hand and up my arm.

Just as I retrieved what looked like a small round gem the beam of colored light snapped out. A loud screech pierced my ears. Quickly, I put the item in the front pocket of my jean shorts.

Uh oh, the real Mama has returned. I scrambled down the tree dodging the egret as she darted her beak at me. I made it down the tree to the boat, and she swooped over me pecking me hard on the head while I untied the boat. Pushing off I called to her, "Go check your babies; they are hungry."

I paddled as fast as I could back in the direction I came from. Calling into the sky. "I have no idea where I am!" No response. I aimlessly paddled for a while. Drifting, I took out the gem and examined it closely. It was very beautiful and shimmered in the sunlight like an opal. The whirr of a fan engine caught my attention. I paddled toward the sound.

Rounding the bend, I could see it was Charlie. Once we made eye contact, he shook his head with his soft locks tossing around his face. I gave him a sheepish grin and a quick rolling finger wave. Not saying a word, he tied my boat to his and extended his arm with an open palm inviting me to climb aboard. The fan on the back of his boat propelled us forward on the water toward Aunt Nina's camp. I watched my little boat dance behind us. Feeling Charlie's eyes watching me, I looked toward him with my shoulders pinned to my ears.

His brow clenched in the middle of his forehead asking me what I was thinking going off like that? I gave him a little shrug and another sheepish grin. He shook his head, taking his gaze from me to look in the direction he was steering the boat. The roar of the fan made it impossible to talk, giving me some time to think about the gem. I wondered if it would fit in the lock to open Aunt Nina's book. *Only one way to find out, but first I must get it back.*

Once we tied up the boats, I followed Charlie up to Aunt Nina's camp, "How long do you plan on staying at Aunt Nina's camp," I asked, ignoring the conversation I knew he wanted to have. Without Charlie's help I could have been lost out there for a long time.

"I may head home and check on things tomorrow. What are your plans?"

"My plan is to get my books back, but I don't know how."

"You do think Father Verum has them? Could you talk to Father Beau?" Charlie quizzed.

"I don't know who to trust and I need some answers."

"Aunt Nina trusted them both, maybe you should just talk to them. If he really did take it, there must be a good reason," Charlie said.

"I tried, but Father and Mr. Wolf basically gave me up as a sacrifice to Madame Fia."

"True, but you didn't really get to talk to Father Verum, did you?"

"No," I agreed with him.

Charlie gently took my hand in his and locked eyes with me, "Arielle, you are stronger than you think. And everyone knows it but you. When are you going to start believing in yourself?"

"I am more confident." I shrugged and looked away. "I miss her, I had so much more to learn from your Aunt."

"Maybe. But you of all people know she will visit you and still help you from the other side."

"She did come to me last night," I said with a longing tone, "but it isn't the same."

He squeezed my hands and let them go, "That's great! Come on, let's keep going through her home looking for anything you may want to keep as a memento."

The night passed quickly. I filled a small brown paper bag with the tea tins that she shared with me on my first visit here, the salve that helped my demon burns, and a coffee mug that reminded me of her. I didn't know what else to take, there might be something of real help, but I didn't want to take things to just take them.

Charlie tied my boat to his and we placed our items in the airboat. Glancing up at the camp as he turned on the fan and engine, I caught a glimpse of a yellow light shining from the front room window. The light cast the shape of a cross dancing on the glass. I smiled knowing she was safe with Jesus. The light flashed once and faded back into the dark room as we pushed off, heading to Charlie's camp.

Gathering our belongings to disembark at Charlie's camp he placed his rugged hand on my forearm to get my attention and asked, "Do you want me to take you to Father Verum?"

Showing the fear in my eyes, "Yes, I would like that," I said softly.

"Okay, first thing tomorrow we will go talk to him," he said sternly.

Swallowing hard, "Might as well."

CHAPTER SIX
Getting Some Answers

Early the next morning, I left my new treasures at Charlie's camp before heading out in his airboat. I kept the gem in the front pocket of my jeans. The bag I carried everywhere was lighter because it only contained my books and Madame Fia's book.

Father Verum's house was a little further boat ride than Aunt Nina's place and down a different waterway. The water frequently changed the course of the inlets and passageways, but it did not phase Charlie and he navigated the route with ease. Charlie has evolved with the swamp. I glanced over at him examining his face, the stiff visor shielded his eyes from the glare of the sun bouncing off the water. His brown corduroy jacket billowed in the wind behind him.

He was so adorable and rugged. I felt the rush of heat fill my cheeks in contrast to the cold. Looking away so he didn't see, I wrapped my arms around my fluffy coat to try to keep my body warm from going in the breeze. My lips started to get colder from the constant wind. I tried to curl them in and cup my gloves around them pushing a deep breath out. It did help, but as soon as I breathed in the cold returned. The boat slowed and leaned forward as we stopped in the water at Father's pier.

Before I could even lean over to grab ahold of the dock, Charlie was airborne and tying us up. He extended his hand to help me out of the boat. I looked up at him and found the way the sunlight shown around his locks and his big grin to be so inviting. Smiling, I successfully grabbed his hand and held tight without pulling us into the freezing waters.

"I got your back, Arielle. And your front," he joked trying to lighten my tense mood, kissing me softly.

I giggled a little. Straightening up and wagging my finger at him, "Charlie this is serious. I need to be in good head space to get my books back. No distractions!" He raised his hands up as if I was pointing a gun at him, "Yes, ma'am." Straight faced he waved for me to take the lead ahead of him.

Tapping on the wooden back door, I immediately turned to Charlie, "No answer, I guess we should go."

"No, we came all this way. What are you afraid of?" he said, wrapping his arm around my waist, spinning me to face the door.

"Uh. Everything, don't you remember the story I just told you about the flames and Madame Fia?"

The door creaked open. I pulled back in surprise, "Mr. Wolf?"

Charlie looked at me in surprise and back at Mr. Wolf waiting for his response.

"Father was wondering when you would show up here, so he asked me to hang out until you did," Mr. Wolf explained.

"Where is he?" I asked with a little more annoyance in my voice than I planned.

"He had to run into town again. He will be back before dark."

I sighed, turning to Charlie, "Now what?"

"We wait," Charlie responded.

"I guess I could find some tea." Mr. Wolf waved for us to come in. Turning around he his cupped hands over his ears pushing the wiry hair back.

Awkwardly we sat around the kitchen table glancing around at the room in front of us until I blurted out, "This is ridiculous. Why don't you answer some of my questions while we wait?"

Mr. Wolf stammered, "I guess I could." He wrung his hands together like he did back in the Egret's Nest. Finally focusing on me, he began the conversation with one word "Shoot."

"Um..." Surprised he agreed, I searched my thoughts with where to start. "Okay for starters, do you have my Papa's book or Aunt Nina's book?"

"Nope. Next?" Mr. Wolf leaned back, pleased with his answer and building confidence. He swung his arm to rest his shoulder over the back of the modest chair.

"Did you take the books from me in the courtyard?"

He tapped his chin and looked up at the ceiling, "Ah. Perhaps?"

"I will take that as a yes." With clenched teeth and disgust, I said, "You could have killed me leaving me there knocked out, ya know."

"Perhaps," he said with a smirk and shrug.

"What was Father trying to sell you?"

"Random stuff," Mr. Wolf smirked.

"I know you are not who you say you are."

"I never told you who I am" he confidently replied.

"I know you wanted me to open Madame Fia's book."

"Yes, that is true." He finally admitted to something.

"But why?" I asked, leaning in.

"Oh, child you are so green," his lips curled as he chuckled, "You don't understand the powers behind each book."

"Yes, I do," I said defensively, "I have learned all kinds of new spells from Papa's book."

He slapped his palm on the table causing the teapot and cups to jump, "Spells! You don't know anything about spells." As his anger seeped out, fur began to grow on his cheeks. "You want to know why I need her book?" he asked, leaning in closer to my face.

I watched Charlie stiffen next to me waiting for the next move. With crossed arms I leaned back away from him, "Yes, I do want to know."

"Some spells are revealed to you in human form and as an individual. But you have not seen the magnitude of spells." Calming himself, he breathed out a long sigh. His breath swirled in a red circle and evaporated.

Unfolding my arms, I cupped my elbows waiting to hear more.

"You are very powerful, and you are part of something larger." He cupped the area where his breath disappeared, collecting it and tossing it above the table. The world around us cracked revealing darkness. Fear crept in as Charlie and the room were now gone, but a small red glow flickered between us, "Why don't you team up with me?" he suggested. He ran his hand around the glow picking it up and holding it close to his face showing his long ears and teeth in full wolf form.

"This isn't real," I said, trying to convince us both I wasn't scared.

"Oh, I am real," he assured me. "There's a lot I can teach you."

"I don't trust you," I said firmly.

"Do you trust Father?" he asked coyly.

"Well, I…" stammering, "I mean for the most part."

"Do you think he will teach you everything you need to know?" He spoke confidently, shaking his head, "I don't think so."

I glanced around, "I'll find my new teacher, somewhere" my voice trailing off.

48

"What can I do to convince you to come with me?"

"Answer my questions," I demanded.

"Very well. It's just you and me, ask away." He tossed the glowing circle filling the area around us.

"Okay, why are you a wolf?"

"I have a genetic mutation and I get hairy sometimes."

"You are so full of crap. See, this is why I can't trust you." I rolled my eyes and glared at him.

"Hey, don't speak to your elders that way!" He shouted pointing his index finger in my face.

"Let me out of here. Now."

"You figure it out." He said leaning back in his chair.

I stood and swung my arms at the air as Mr. Wolf chuckled and gradually transformed back into the clerk.

I sat back down folding my arms, I leaned back in my chair repeating to myself *This isn't real.*

Mr. Wolf smirked, saying, "Give up child? See, you do need me."

I turned my focus away from him and stared beyond the red glow. I slowed my breathing. Charlie came into focus. As I whispered, "He's right there."

Mr. Wolf tried to break my concentration and instill fear, "You cannot get out of here without me. You need me."

"You have no power over me, this isn't real." I stood and faced Charlie who was frozen in his chair and becoming clearer to me as the redness dimmed.

"No, no, no. You need me," Mr. Wolf said, standing and lunging at me.

I raised my palm and a blue bubble popped out blocking him from touching me. The room came back into full color and focus. Charlie was still frozen in time. Mr. Wolf fanatically swiped at the bubble. As I calmly walked to Charlie and touched his cheek. He gasped for air looking at me, "You were just sitting here," He pointed to my chair. How did you get here?"

Turning my head toward Mr. Wolf who was standing still, "He is a liar," I said with clenched teeth as the bubble popped between us.

"What happened?" Charlie asked.

"I was just telling Arielle the truth and she doesn't want to hear it," Mr. Wolf explained to Charlie.

"I just want my damn books back!" I exclaimed.

"I bet you do," Father Verum said while stepping into the kitchen. "But there is no reason to be hostile in my home."

"Father, we have been waiting for you," I said, softening my tone, but not apologizing for my words looking down at my now folded hands. I became a little child in my mind all over again, being fussed at by a priest for talking to the dead.

"I figured you would show up after our little encounter the other night. Charlie, how are you?" Father asked, nodding toward him.

"I am making do with the new events in my life." Charlie continued, "Current project is helping Arielle get her Papa's and my Aunt's books back. Enough of the charades. Do you have them?"

"I do not have them. I told her when she asked before," Father said dryly.

"I know Mr. Wolf took them from me in the courtyard, but you were the only person who knew I would be there," I stated.

"I did go to the courtyard, but you were not there, and neither was Mr. Wolf for that matter."

"Wait, you didn't see me laying in the courtyard?" I blinked confused.

"No, when I got there, it was empty," he confessed.

I spun to face Mr. Wolf pointed at him as little blue sparks sputtered from my fingertip, "You! You did this to me." Looking down I recalled the memory out loud, "Wait, there was this weird bubble encasing me." Turning back to Father, "So you didn't see me at all or anything?"

Father shook his head and locked eyes with me. *How can I trust him when he is hanging out with Mr. Wolf?*

"I am so over this. Charlie, let's go."

Charlie gently grabbed my arm and whispered, "We came all his way. Is there anything else you want to ask Father?"

Taking a deep breath I nodded, "Yes, I do need some answers."

"Come sit." He pointed to the table. Then turning to Mr. Wolf, "Thank you. You are excused."

Mr. Wolf snarled, but obeyed Father retreating to another room.

"Why is he even here?" I pointed in the direction Mr. Wolf left.

Father leaned in and spoke quietly, "I need him to accomplish something. I cannot explain it right now. Trust me, I'm trying to protect you. You are just a child and you have so much power you don't know what to do with it, especially with the books. It is dangerous," he gently warned me.

Puffing up, "I'll determine what I need and don't need. Those were my books. They were given to me. You are not my Papa. You don't even know me." Little blue streaks of light spit from my fingertips.

Pointing to my hands, "See you can't control yourself. Exactly why you don't need that much power. I can help you, but you have to trust me right now."

"I'm out of here, this is not worth my time." I grabbed Charlie's arm to pull him to follow me out but crumbled to the floor when a shock escaped my hand. "Oh Charlie, I am so sorry!" I knelt next to him, locking my fingers to not touch him.

"See, you can't control your powers. You need help Arielle," Mr. Wolf chuckled from the doorway.

Father jumped up, walking over to scold Mr. Wolf, "I asked you to leave."

Spinning around, "You're not helping! This is all your fault. If you wouldn't have taken the books in the first place this would not be happening." A deep blue bubble pulsed from me colliding with Father and Mr. Wolf sending them crashing to the ground. Mr. Wolf transformed back into wolf form and whimpered like a dog. My anger grew and I posed to send another shock from my joined palms.

From the ground Father weakly raised his palm, and recited:

"Spirits hear my call,

Make her powers small.

Just for a moment,

To me bestow."

A soft purple mist covered me, freezing my body and my powers as I slumped to the floor.

Recovering from the blue shock, Charlie ran to me scooping me up into his arms. "Charlie, I feel funny. I can't see you," I said with a slur. My eyes searched for him to come into focus.

"I've got you, Arielle. What did you do to her?" Charlie said, demanding an answer.

Mr. Wolf and Father both stood a little wobbly. "I only stunned her powers. The effects only last a few minutes. She needed to calm down."

"You are going to pay for this," I slurred.

"You left me no choice. Our visit's over. She's too dangerous and is not welcome here," Father said to Charlie pointing toward the door with his arm shaking.

Charlie carried me out and down the stairs to the boat. I was able to climb into the air boat and take my seat. "Do you want to wait a few minutes before we take off?" Charlie asked.

Looking up at the house, we could see Father and the wolf watching us from the window. I flicked my fingers toward them. A blue streak popped out but did not go far enough to clear the pier.

"Okay then, I think we should just go now before you blow up the whole house," Charlie said, cranking up the fan, and we whizzed away. We rode in silence all the way back.

I plopped down on a kitchen chair watching Charlie, still not saying anything. Charlie joined me at the kitchen. Placing our coffee and a plate of blueberry muffins between us. He asked, "Why are you so angry?"

"Why shouldn't I be? I'm angry because I lost the books. I'm upset because I can't talk to Papa or Aunt Nina. I need help, but not the kind of help Father or that stupid Wolf is offering. This is all their fault."

"Arielle, you are becoming more powerful. You're very angry. You're new to all of this, you might need to be still and find your center before you hurt someone," Charlie suggested.

"So, I am not allowed to be angry?" I asked with daggers.

"You are allowed, but that won't bring anyone back or find the books. Why don't you go lie down?" he suggested.

I sighed, "Okay," submitting to his request.

Once I was comfortably in bed I fell into a deep slumber. Creatures crept into my world carrying me away from Charlie's and we flew into the cold night sky. The stars whizzed by like lightning bolts around me. The winged creatures dropped me gently and disappeared. I was standing in the swamp by Aunt Nina's camp. "Hello?" I called. The darkness was lit by the stars filling the sky with no clouds. The moon was a medium size silver with a slight haze around it. My eyes adjusted looking for anyone coming to visit me.

A pink cloud formed into a tornado tunnel from the heavens. It moved down the ground then evaporated to reveal Aunt Nina. In a second cloud tunnel, which was navy blue in color, Papa appeared. Then in a third cloud tunnel that was orange stood Madame Fia with a scowl. "Really? You? You are here to ruin my experience. Couldn't you find someone else to annoy?" I asked Madame Fia.

Aunt Nina touched my shoulder. "Child, you should be kind to all spirits."

"She tried to kill me!" I whined.

"Madame, would you please explain your position?" Aunt Nina called to her.

"You disturbed my slumber. I must fulfill the request before I can return. Why did you wake me?" she asked me just like she did before.

I turned to Papa, "I don't know what she wants from me. I didn't wake her on purpose if I did wake her at all. What should I do?"

Papa spoke, "My beautiful Arielle, I wish we would have more time together. Our time tonight is short as well." He touched my cheek with his hand.

Aunt Nina continued, "You have great powers, but you will need the help from the three of us to get the books back. You need Madame Fia to help you locate the books. Madame represents fire, I'm the waters, your Papa is the earth, you are the wind. Ask Madame to join us."

"Okay, but she did try to kill me," I said with my hand on my hip. "Madame, will you please help us find their books?" I curiously asked.

"Yes, let us commence so I may return to my slumber," she said, examining her nails that were little orange flames.

Papa took a wide stance raising his palms up arms out wide as if he were holding a huge beach ball. Aunt Nina did the same about 6 feet away. Madame repeated the same motions. They all turned looking at me to do the same. Taking the last spot to complete our circle my palms raised to meet the same height as the others. Completing the circle, we formed one crystal ball from our feet extending way over our heads.

Papa called out, "Earth." The ball filled with dark mud.

Aunt Nina called out, "Water." The mud was washed to one side of the ball both taking up equal parts.

Madame called out, "Fire." Blazes of fire filled the section next to the mud pushing the water over making the ball fill with 3 equal parts. All three gazed at me through the translucent ball filled with their talents.

I called out, "Wind." Air pulled from my body filling the last part of the ball creating four equal parts of earth, water, fire, and wind.

Papa recited, "Once was lost, now is found. Once was stolen, now is returned. Bless this child, visions of the lost."

The ball swirled with the four elements. A pulse of images formed. The books appeared one by one, first Papa's leather book and popped out of view then Aunt Nina's book was shown then disappeared abruptly. Fire took over the ball, then water extinguished it. The ball spun with water as if shaking a water bottle in a circle, the water clung to the edges showing the center empty. Darkness filled the ball as the water drained out. The darkness had a texture with wiry lines of black, dark brown and a little grey. The ball spun and the rotation slowed revealing the face of Mr. Wolf.

Gasping for air I ripped myself from the dream, "Charlie!" I screamed.

He came stumbling into the guest room, "What? What is it?" He mumbled with sleep still in his eyes.

"He still has my books!"

"That's great Arielle, but we can't do anything about it at this time of night. Well actually morning, 3 in the morning," he rambled half asleep, "Wait! You know who it is?"

"Yes! I was still, well I was asleep, but I got the help I needed to figure it out."

"Is it Father?"

"No. It's that lying clerk, Mr. Wolf. He is the owner of the Egret's Nest shop."

"I guess you are going back to the city tomorrow?" he asked while yawning.

"You're coming with me?" I pleaded.

"Arielle, you know I support you in everything, but you don't need me. With your powers you don't need me to protect you. We will talk more in the morning. Try to get some real sleep this time. Good night."

Darkness enveloped the room and I felt calm as I used my thoughts to call out to my three helpers. *Sorry I didn't stay longer but thank you for your help and guidance. Madame Fia, I hope you can return to your slumber now. Papa, I love you and miss you. I have so many questions for you! Aunt Nina, thank you for continuing to protect and guide me. I look forward to seeing you again soon.*

CHAPTER SEVEN
A Wolf to Capture

The next morning, I called Mama to tell her I was coming home. Charlie suggested I leave Aunt Nina's treasures at his place since I was determined to go straight to the shop. I did not need any more baggage.

I bundled up and Charlie gave me a warm kiss for the trip home. Charlie waved from his porch calling, "Arielle, I believe in you. Just don't let your emotions take over." he warned.

"Thank you, Charlie, I'll try," I said leaving the warmth of his hug.

I parked the motorcycle outside of the shop. Grabbing the door handle I jiggled it and found it wouldn't turn. My fist rapped hard on the door, rattling it with each pound. I waited a few seconds before pounding another time.

"Who is out there?" a muffled voice called.

"You know who it is Mr. Wolf, open up."

"We are closed, come back when we open at 10," The voice responded.

"I'm not leaving!"

"I'm going to call the police."

"Call the police so you can explain why you stole my books!"

The door creaked open revealing a little hunched man, "Dear, I didn't steal anything, and I'll call the cops!"

"Wait, who are you?" I blinked rapidly in confusion.

"I own this shop, who are you?"

"I must be mistaken. I am looking for a clerk with a beret and wiry hair. Doesn't he work here?"

"I don't know what you are talking about. Please come back at 10 if you want to shop." I stood there flabbergasted with a dropped jaw as he firmly shut the door in my face.

What now? Glancing up looking for a sign from above I saw it. Etched into the eves was a very small wood carving of a symbol I'd seen once before at my own home! Half "N" and half of a "D". My palm slapped my forehead a little too hard causing it to sting.

This is a dwelling place of both demons and angels, you idiot, I scolded myself. *Mr. Wolf was not really here the other day. He created a covering to trick me while I was in the shop the other day.* Stomping my foot on the concrete releasing my anger, the brick smashed under the blue electricity that escaped my foot. I took a few deep breaths and thought to myself. *Calm yourself! Maybe it is time to find Father Beau and ask him some questions. There are signs and symbols all around us guiding us, I just need to pay closer attention. I kept getting wrapped up in myself and not seeing the big picture.*

Returning to my motorcycle I drove home to eat and get cleaned up making the trip across town to Father Beau's chapel. Once the motorcycle was parked in the courtyard, I dismounted. The side door was unlocked. I went in and dropped my items on the coffee table then collapsed on the couch thinking about all the events from the last few days. Mama came into the room and tapped my legs to get me to move. Swinging them toward the ceiling, she sat on the couch, and I gently put my legs on her lap. Not even opening my eyes I said, "Hi Mama."

"Hi Arielle. How was your trip to see Charlie?"

"It was good, I felt better after seeing him."

"That's good. I am sure you two have not been watching the news," she suggested patting my legs.

"No. Why?" I moved my arm from across my eyes and glanced at her. Looking for a reaction since her voice wasn't giving anything away.

"You might want to call Charlie and give him a heads up."

Pushing up on my elbows to see her, "Why? What is going on?"

"A hurricane is on its way, it was going toward Pensacola, but it has turned heading straight for us. Looks like it will make landfall tonight. Category 2 might even be a 3. He can come here to be safer than out in the swamp."

I jumped up and darted to the phone in the kitchen. Spinning the dial on the old phone I selected his number. The phone rang, no answer. Not this again. I called again, no answer. Moving quickly back to the couch. I sat next to Mama. "I must go back and warn him. He isn't answering the phone."

"Young lady, you are going nowhere. We have to prepare the house and the tide is rising already you could easily get lost on the water with everything looking different. Just keep calling him. You know he is prepared for this sort of thing living on the water."

"But Mama," I whined, tears welling up in my eyes.

"Call him again. Then come help me get the plywood stacked up in the attic to start boarding up the windows."

60

I called again with no answer. A category 3 hurricane would be very severe. I didn't even ask what side of the storm we were on or how fast it was moving. That makes a difference as well. The east side always gets a lot more rain. New Orleans is below sea level, so we basically live in a giant soup bowl. Any long downpours can fill up the drainage system quickly and flood houses. We are in a decent area, and to my knowledge the house has never flooded. Helping Mama lug the large sheets of plywood to the windows was quite a chore. Mark and Papa were both here the last time we had to board up the windows. This was a new challenge for the both of us.

Mama was stronger than I thought she would be, which made it easier for the two of us to place the wood. I leaned in with my palms square on the board as Mama twisted the latches. Three on each side to keep the boards secure and protect the windows from any projectile items the storm might toss at our home.

Once we secured the last board, 22 in total, we moved down the stairs to the second floor. This was much easier to board up because Mama had storm shutters installed on this level. Once the accordion metal shutters were finally locked in place, we made our way downstairs to the first level to complete our task.

Meeting Mama in the kitchen she said, "Thank you, I really couldn't do this without you."

"You are welcome," I said, going back to the phone to call Charlie again.

"Hello?"

"Charlie! Oh, thank God you answered."

"Hey glad you made it home, everything going okay?"

"No, not really. Did you know Hurricane Olga's path changed? She's on her way here."

"Oh crap, no. I have been so busy with you and everything at Aunt Nina's house that I am totally out of my routine of listening to the radio news every morning."

"She might be Cat 3. Are you going to be okay? Can you come here?"

Mama whispered to me, "It's a slow-moving storm and we are going to be on the wet side, tell him to come here."

"Mama said you have to come here," I said before he could even answer me. "After the storm you can help me with that… project we were talking about," I said, dropping my voice on the last part.

Mama whispered, "What project?"

"Don't ask. It's a surprise," I said, holding my hand over the receiver so Charlie couldn't hear me.

"Are you still talking to me or your Mama?"

"Hey Charlie, yes I'm talking to you." I frantically waved at Mama to give me some privacy.

"Tell him to come here," Mama yelled loudly as she walked out of the kitchen.

"Did you hear her?" I asked him.

"Yes, I hear her, but I'm not coming. My house is safe, and I need to keep an eye on things here."

"But you'll lose power, how will I get a hold of you? And I won't know if you are safe," I whined.

"That is just the chance you will have to take. Seriously, Arielle, you know I am equipped to handle any category hurricane." he assured me.

"I know I'm not going to convince you otherwise. I will just be worried the whole time."

"Trust me. Hey, did you go see Father Beau? Or meet up with Mr. Wolf?" Charlie asked, changing the subject.

"No, Mama had me helping her get the house boarded up. It's getting dark soon. I guess after the storm. And another peculiar thing, Mr. Wolf doesn't work at the shop. There was some old man who didn't have any clue who Mr. Wolf was. He tricked me and now I don't know how to find him."

"Why am I not surprised? Look, I have some things to do to prep for the storm. I'll talk to you later. And don't worry I'm a pro at this. Talk to you soon. Okay?"

"Okay, be careful. I'll call you tonight. Is your answering machine broken? It never seems to pick up when I call?"

"Yeah, it stopped working a few weeks ago, I haven't gotten a new one."

"Well, that's dumb. You need a new one."

"I'll get that right after Olga passes."

"Good! Alright, I'll let you go."

"Talk to you soon."

Once settled for the night I placed the small gem I found in the Egret's Nest on my dresser. "We'll have to figure out what you're all about another time, won't we," I told them. I headed downstairs to eat some hurricane food with Mama and see how the night would unfold.

CHAPTER EIGHT

Olga In the Night

For some unknown reason hurricanes always seemed to pass in the middle of the night and Olga was no exception. Mama and I had a spread of snacks while we waited for Olga's appearance. Chips, candy, popcorn, bread, peanut butter, brownies, ice cream and bottled water. We filled the tubs with water in case we lost power and water pressure. We could use the water from the tubs to flush the toilets. Lots of little tricks have been learned over the years.

Mama and I sat in the living room each with our little pint of ice cream for dinner. I picked mint chocolate chip and she picked vanilla. We chatted about family up north as the rain started to patter harder outside. Mama clicked on the television to watch our favorite weatherman Rob Wreck. Mama joked "Wob Wreck is about to give an update and wreck our weekend!" Speaking like she had a lisp pronouncing his name. I laughed and turned my focus to the tv.

He announced, pointing to the map behind him, "Well folks, it looks like we're in for a long night. I'll be here all night keeping close watch on Olga. The low-lying areas already know she's here. The water levels are rising fast. So, I hope you have prepared yourself for a wet, rainy night."

Jumping off the couch I pattered over to the phone, "Charlie, Wob Wreck is on. He said things are already amping up by you. Is that true?"

"Don't you mean Rob Wreck?" He corrected.

"Sorry inside joke with Mama and me. How's the water there?"

"It's climbing, and the dock is already underwater."

"I told you, you should have come here!"

"Arielle, and I told you I am safe. Stop worrying. Go back to eating your hurricane snacks." He said, then deflecting with a question, "What are you eating first?"

"Ice cream of course. If we lose power, it will melt."

"So true. Enjoy your ice cream. Try to get some sleep tonight."

"I doubt that will happen. Goodnight."

"Goodnight."

I hung up the phone and just stared at the wall. Mama placed her hand on my shoulder and gave it a light squeeze. "Your ice cream is melting. Come back and sit down."

"I'm not hungry."

"Come sit with me anyway. We can find a movie on television."

I settled next to her on the couch and pulled up the full blanket to get comfortable as she clicked away with the remote. "Oh, this looks interesting. Ghostbusters."

I gave her a side glance. Is she mocking me? Nope, she is all smiles and completely into the selections, "Sounds great Mama. I'll go get the popcorn."

"Thanks sweetie. We only have a few minutes before it starts, so hurry back."

"That was an interesting take on busting ghosts," I said to Mama before realizing she had her head back and mouth open with a slight snore. I took the popcorn bowl from her hand and quietly placed it on the coffee table. My helmet and bag still lay there from earlier. Was it just a few hours since I put them down, seems like almost a week. I was exhausted.

I gingerly walked to the front door to peek out the glass trying to see how the weather was picking up. The winds were pushing the heavy rain sideways. The streets were starting to fill with water a little. We still had hours more of this, so I was glad to see the drainage system was keeping up so far.

Returning back to Mama I tapped her on the shoulder and whispered, "Mama? I am tired, you want to go to bed?"

She smacked her lips closed and open a few times. "Sure." Making her way up the stairs for the night she paused remembering we had not cleaned up our snacks.

"Go up, I've got this." I gathered our bowls and other left-over snack items. Leaving them in the kitchen sink, I ran to answer the phone. "Hey, you stud muffin!" I answered jokingly.

"I didn't know you thought that much of me," Mark replied.

"Oh, it's just you. How's the family, bro?" I asked.

"Fine, just checking in on y'all. Sounds like we are going to get hammered with the weather. We only have a little rain so far."

"Yeah, but it's starting to pick up," I said with a sigh.

"I take it you couldn't convince Charlie to come stay with y'all?"

"Nope."

"He's a smart guy; he will be fine," Mark assured me.

"I know, but I still will worry. I learned that from Mama."

"Yes, you did. Hey, did you go talk to Father Verum?" he asked.

"Sounds like you've been talking to Charlie. Yes, I have and there are some new developments. I'm just trying to sort everything out now. I need to go see Father Beau when this storm is over."

"Ah okay, I was just curious if there was any progress. Tell Mama I love her, and I'll call in the morning. Stay safe."

"Love ya too, night." I was glad that Mark knew all the crazy things going on in my life and could help navigate things with me from time to time.

Mama was already tucked in bed with her door shut. I didn't want to wake her to tell her Mark called. I can do that in the morning. Settling in bed, I closed my eyes and prayed. *God keep all those I know and love safe tonight. Amen.*

Lights flashed illuminating my room and my new little gem pulsed with each flash. The strong winds hollered outside my window. I understand the concept of a storm window, but it doesn't help that you are kept blind and wondering what is going on out there. I crept downstairs to peek out the front door. Huge sheets of rain swept down the street. Someone's aluminum trash can blew past the front door. It was really getting rough out there.

Just as I was thinking *we still had electricity and I could call Charlie*, the power flickered off and, on several times, then leaving me in darkness. *Brilliant, Arielle, you totally spoke that into existence.* Carefully climbing the stairs in the dark, I made it to my room and found my flashlight. Clicking it on, the room filled with a soft, thin yellow light. I clicked it off to save the battery and curled back into bed.

"Ariellllle…" My eyes fluttered open, focusing in the dark. The room lit up for a couple of seconds revealing a glimpse of several creatures in my bedroom. The lightning flashed showing the creatures were still there but had moved to different positions around the room. I held my breath and clicked the flashlight on. The long beam shot through the darkness, allowing me to search the room, but I didn't spot any more creatures. I clicked the flashlight off and pulled the covers up to my nose and waited. The lightning did a triple flash revealing that the creatures congregated around my bed. At the foot of the bed on the left was a ram with a pig's snout. Next to him stood a rabbit-eared, deer looking animal on two legs. Quickly clicking the flashlight on, I shined the beam at them. They were not there anymore.

"What do you want?" I whispered to them.

"Your presence is requested outside of this dwelling." The rabbit pronounced the letter "S" with a long hissing sound.

"You do know there is a CAT 3 hurricane outside, right?" I said a little coyly.

"You either come or we will take you. Your choice." The ram's voice was jumpy and deep.

"It's not the CAT 3 that you are used to," the rabbit said. "You say CAT for category, but CAT really means Crusade Among Terrene. Come, you will see."

Pulling the covers back dramatically I placed my feet into my slippers on the floor. The walls fell back, and the floor dropped out as if a pin were taken out of a door. I began falling into darkness. A large, winged creature scooped me into his arms. I rocked in his arms with each large pump of his wings.

"What's happening? And what does Crusade Among Terrene, even mean?" I asked him. Not answering, he carried me over to a flat rock and deposited me gently. Taking flight, it left me all alone. Glancing around my new surroundings I was thankful for the long flickers of the lightning helped my vision.

Sounds of swords clashing filled my ears. Animal grunts and howls filled the rainy night. Straining to see what was happening in the middle of the hurricane, I noticed that each time a bird flew by a huge gust of wind followed.

Two birds in flight were fighting and ran smack into a tree lifting it up with them. The roots dangled with clumps of dirt flying all around. A sword pierced the creatures and blood poured out spraying around. The tree plummeted back down toward the ground below. The victorious bird flew to me and grabbed me by the arms with his talons. I firmly held onto his legs creating a second grip. Gliding down in the darkness, I saw my street. The tree was lodged into the neighbor's roof about three blocks away.

My feet dangled as we made our descent. The creature hovered over the street releasing me. I released my hold, landing flat-footed on the ground, my knees buckling upon impact with the street. Scrambling up I called to him, "What is happening?"

He flew away into the night sky screeching loudly. "Hello? Anyone going to help me out here?" I stood outside my completely locked house. The storm was intensifying. Up and down the street pairs of creatures were engaged in battle. Shielding my eyes from the wind and rain I could not believe what I was seeing. I didn't understand what this battle was and why it was going on during a hurricane. Slowly I started to see more and more of them and less of the storm. Where I would normally see gusts of wind, it was replaced by winged creatures. Falling trees from a tornado were the unfortunate casualty of a fight. Instead of rain I could see blood spilling from the wounds of creatures. Lightning bolts were creatures tragically falling to the earth in death. Sparks from swords clashing would briefly illuminate the night sky. I think I was witnessing another dimension. It appears that these fights translate to us as a storm.

Luckily, I was not directly a part of this fight, but seeing this opened my eyes to what else might be happening under the surface of what I normally see. I continued to watch, trying to figure out what they were fighting for. I wasn't even sure which team I would be on if I needed to help at some point. The "storm" continued as I pressed my body against the outside of my home trying to stay out of the line of vision.

A fire-breathing dragon flew by methodically searching for something. I stepped away from my house to watch him from the sidewalk. The iridescent green scales flashed from the nearby "lightning". He was so beautiful I just wanted to touch him. He paused in the sky and let out a cannon ball of fire igniting the small restaurant

69

with an apartment upstairs. A family screamed pouring out in the street. All they could see was the fire, not the dragon perched on the building across the street watching the havoc.

What a jerk! The family pulled a hose out trying to douse the restaurant with water in hopes of extinguishing the bright orange and red flickering flames engulfing the roof shingles and fascia. The dragon pushed off his perch and disappeared into the sky. The people were able to put out the flames and hurried back inside just as a sword dug into another creature pouring "rain" down upon them. My stomach turned a little seeing the bright red blood sprinkle over the people. *What is the point of me seeing this?* I questioned.

A white fluffy dog jogged down the street toward me. "Breeze? Is that you?" I called to him. I was so happy to see my spirit animal. He always helped guide me whenever I was not sure what to do or what direction to take. Kneeling as he approached, I wrapped my arms around his neck. I was pretty sure he was also my Papa. "I am so glad to see you," I said, releasing his neck. The wet drops of blood showed up against his stark white fur. "I don't think it's safe for me to be out here, can you help me?" He started to trot down the street toward Royal Street. I followed closely behind him, squishing in my slippers. We stopped in front of The Egret's Nest shop. "Really? This place again?"

His nose practically touching the door seemed like a yes to me. I gave the door knob a twist. The brassy knob lit up as beams of light shined through the frame and keyhole. The door opened, the wind howled, and all the commotion behind me stopped. It was just as calm as the eye of the storm was passing over us. Breeze entered the room which was filled with blinding white light and I followed. The door slammed shut behind us. The room fell into darkness.

I crouched down and felt for Breeze. He was right there with me. As my eyes adjusted, I could see a brown wooden pedestal in the middle of the room. Something was on top of it. I rose and walked to the pedestal. It was a leather book. It was Papa's book! Reaching for the book my hands went right through it. Sadly, it was just an illusion.

Spinning around, I searched the room for Breeze. He sat by the front door watching me. I stood firmly and very still placing my hands around the edges of the closed book. It was still a mirage. *Be still and let your light shine.* My hands filled with a soft rainbow of colors encompassing the book. Standing as still as I could I waited. I focused on my breathing. Breathe in, breathe out. As time passed, I lightly touched the book with my right index finger. For a split second it was there, then my finger pressed through the mirage.

Be still and let your light shine. It felt like an eternity, but I tried over and over again. This time my finger pressed on the hard leather cover and it remained intact. It was working. It was becoming real. In time I was able to place each finger on the book until my whole hand wrapped around each side.

I could hear the "storm" starting up again. The eye of the storm must have completely passed over. I pulled the book to my chest and held it tightly. It was real; I had it back! Breeze and I exited the Egret's Nest back onto the street. There were more creatures all around us fighting furiously. The book glowed blue catching the attention of all the creatures near us. Their squawks and howls filled the night air. A group tried to keep the creatures back while they pressed to get closer to me. Breeze nudged me to move with his snout. I kicked off my slippers and darted down the street. Spilled blood filled the street from wounded creatures. I clung to the book and scurried on.

Getting closer to the house, I saw Breeze right ahead of me, he was completely red from the "rain". I pulled on the front door, but it was locked. Creatures began to close in on us. Breeze stood in front of me with drenched fur standing up on his back as much as possible. Breeze lunged at one of the six-eyed creatures with wings. It swung one of its four arms making contact with Breeze. He yelped and flew into me. My wet hand dropped the book onto the ground. As it bounced and the book flopped open. A blue beam of light shot into the sky. Breeze used his whole body, pushing me into the beam. Both of us were sucked into the book and it snapped shut.

It was dark. I heard Papa's voice, "Arielle?"

"Papa?"

"Oh, what a pickle you always seem to get yourself into, my daughter," he chuckled.

"I know, why is that?" I whispered. "Where are you? I want to see you."

"The book is closed, so it is dark in here."

"Papa, what does Crusade Among Terrene mean?" I asked into the darkness.

"It can be scary. Crusade Among Terrene basically means you saw a battle of Angels and creatures here on earth." I listened quietly as he continued, "When the time is right you will see more."

"I don't think I wanted to see all of that," I admitted.

"There's always something happening that you might not be able to see with your eyes, because it has yet to be revealed to you."

"Kind of what you're trying to explain to Mama about your book?"

"Yes, she doesn't see the world the same, not everyone is designed to."

"I'm sorry I lost your book," I told him.

"It's not your fault. Evil people will always try to take things that are not theirs."

"Mama was saying something about you being killed because of your research. Is that true?"

"In time all things will be revealed to you, but for now don't worry about it."

72

Changing the subject since he wasn't going to give up any more information I asked, "Papa, why didn't I get hurt in all of the fighting?"

"You are not part of their battle. However, some people can get hurt in the storms and that is a very sad casualty of these fights."

"Why are they fighting on Earth? Can't they just go somewhere else?" I asked Papa.

"From what I have learned the demon and angels come here to battle to create more havoc on Earth. It's time for you to rest, be still and let your light shine," he said to me.

I sat down on the warm ground. I could feel the grass with my fingers, it is dry and soft. "Be still you say, let your light shine you tell me."

"Yes," he whispered to me.

I laid on my back resting my hands on my stomach feeling the rhythm of the rise and fall of my breath. *Let your light shine,* I repeated to myself drifting off to sleep.

CHAPTER NINE

One More Book

Mama's voice seemed muffled, "Wake up sleepy head."

"Mama? Where's Papa? Why are you here?"

"You must have had a doozy of a dream. Papa's gone, sweetie."

"But he was here."

She placed the back of her hand on my forehead, "You are not running a fever," she observed moving her hand to my cheek next. "Are you feeling okay?"

"I don't think I slept well with the storm."

"You should see the tree on the neighbor's roof and the little restaurant with the house upstairs down the way must have caught on fire! I took a little walk this morning to see the damage. We were very lucky here. Although, I think there was a lightning strike right outside our house. There is a rectangle black mark on the sidewalk, very weird."

"That is weird. Did you sleep through it all?" I asked her.

"I didn't even hear the thunder last night. Looks like the city's drainage system worked great. I also called Mark, they did fine at their farm too," Mama told me. "Wob Wreck said we had over 2 feet of rain last night!"

"My head hurts. I'm going to lay here a bit before getting up."

"Sure thing, sweetie. Do you want something for your head?"

"No thanks."

"Okay. Coffee's ready whenever you come downstairs." She pulled my door closed as she left.

I felt around under the covers, my hand touched leather. Pulling it out I laid eyes on it. Papa's book! I got it back in a weird turn of events. The spine made a crack sound as I opened it. The pages easily turned toward the middle end of the book. Looking inside, burn marks along the spine show where 3 pages were removed from the binding.

I sat in bed, legs crossed with the book in my lap, trying to remember what was on those pages. I traced my finger on the spine, thinking hard. I read his book many times, but I couldn't recall if it was a story, a spell or just an event. Gingerly I closed the book gazing at the foot of the bed. Breeze was there, white as snow once again. He whined and walked closer. "Hey buddy, thanks for everything." I cupped his chin in my hand and gave him a little scratch. He curled up next to me and faded away leaving a small dent in the plush comforter where he was lying.

I flopped back in bed and closed my eyes as I tucked the book back under the covers next to me. At least I have Papa's book back. I didn't know why someone would take the pages, and why only those pages? One more thing to figure out, I told myself.

"Arielle?" Mama whispered from the door, "Are you getting up today?"

I groaned from lack of sleep from the busy night. "I just want to sleep Mama."

"Okay. Maybe you can help me with the windows later? Did you call Charlie yet?"

My eyes popped open and I sprung out of bed right over to the phone. Smashing the keys hard, the phone tone registered each number. "Do – Do – Do." The familiar sounds of a disconnected line sounded, "We're sorry please check the number and dial again." The female voice told me. I slammed the phone down and shuffled back to bed.

Mama was still standing in the doorway. "Maybe you can try again later," she suggested. "You know they lose power a lot out at those camps. I'm sure he is fine."

I pulled the covers over my head, "I know Mama, but I'm still worried. Goodnight."

"It's morning, but okay, goodnight." She pulled my door closed and went about her day.

I woke up and realized it was dark outside. I must have slept the whole day. My stomach growled at me for neglecting it. *There were plenty of hurricane snacks leftover* I thought as I eased downstairs into the kitchen. I ate a handful of chips and peeked out the front door. The night was quiet. I dialed Charlie's number again, getting the same recording. I climbed the stairs and drew a hot bath to soak for a while. Then I quietly went back to bed. Since Mama's door was closed, I figured she was already asleep for the night.

The smell of bacon filled my nostrils notifying my stomach it was breakfast time. Rise and shine. I wasn't really sure what day it was, but I remembered I still had not heard from Charlie. Calling from the phone in my room before making my way to the kitchen I leaned against the wall waiting for his calm voice. The phone was ringing, which was a good sign the power was back on. No answer and no answering machine either. I pulled my fuzzy socks over my feet and slowly made my way down the staircase. "Mama?" I called and patted my hair to keep it somewhat in order.

"We're in the kitchen, sweetie."

We? I said to myself as I shuffled down the stairs a little faster, trying to hurry, but not fall with the soft socks on the hard-wooden stairs. Rounding the doorframe into the kitchen my eyes lit up and I slid toward him. "Charlie!" I threw my arms around his neck, tucking my head into his collar. "Holy crap, I've been so worried!"

He gingerly patted my back, "I figured as much. I had to come to town to get some items and I couldn't not check in on you."

"You staying awhile?" I begged folding my hands together with my knuckles intertwined.

76

"I'm staying for breakfast, your Mama insisted," he said.

"I guess I'll take it," I said as I dropped my hands to my sides in sadness.

"I 'm so glad you decided to get up and join us. You would have really been mad if you slept through my visit!" he joked trying to lighten my mood.

Charlie described his hurricane experience at the camp. The winds were bending the trees like pipe cleaners. One of them snapped and splintered, sending shards everywhere, but most of them swayed and danced in the wind.

I wanted to share what I saw, but not in front of Mama. She didn't know all the bizarre things that went on in my life and I would like to protect her by keeping her out of it as much as possible.

Charlie continued and talked about the lightning show with loud cracks of thunder. He too had the eye of the hurricane pass over him. The damage was not too bad. He lost a few boards along the porch that needed to be replaced anyway. The alligators were doing fine, barely noticed anything had even happened.

He didn't make it out to Aunt Nina's yet to take inventory. The waterways were overflowing from the rainwater making everything look different and difficult to navigate. I smiled at him as he talked about the storm, daydreaming about what our lives would be like if I went with him forever or he just stayed in New Orleans.

"Breakfast was delicious. Thank you for the hospitality, but I must be hitting the road."

I poked my bottom lip out forming a frowning face, trying to make my eyes large, "Do you have to go?"

"Who will take care of the alligators?"

"Your cousin Nick?" I suggested.

A single "Ha." Escaped Charlie's mouth, "I don't think so. He has really backed off from the business. He has been doing fishing tours out by the Rigolets and doing very well I might add."

"Really? I didn't know he was doing that."

"Yes, going great. He called it Strictly Business Fishing Charters. I will talk to him if you want to go out one day. He always catches fish: reds, trout, croaker, flounder. And always gets the limit, he really has a knack for it."

"That sounds like fun, I haven't been fishing in forever. We should go!"

Charlie put his plate and coffee mug in the kitchen sink and ran water over it. "Thank you for the breakfast," he said looking at Mama then nodding at me.

"You're always welcome here," Mama said as she went to work on the dishes.

I followed Charlie to the front door and went outside with him. Closing the door completely, "Oh Charlie, I have so much to tell you. When are you coming back?"

"I have quite a bit to repair at the camp, but I need to know if you had any luck getting the books back? Did you see Father Beau?"

"I got Papa's book back, I will have to explain all that later, but there are pages missing. I don't have Aunt Nina's book yet. No, I didn't make it to Father Beau's yet with the storm and all."

"Any ideas how to get her book back?"

"Not yet, but I am working on it. Mr. Wolf's definitely involved somehow."

"Maybe you can come next weekend, the waters should be back to normal by then and we can catch up."

"Okay, I will plan on coming Friday, if I can't get a hold of you on the phone to make sure you are home. And let me know if I need to bring any more supplies."

"That sounds good," he agreed.

"But before you go, I have to tell you the hurricane I experienced was nothing like what we have seen before. There were creatures battling all around us causing the storm." I said, excited to be able to share this with him.

"That's crazy, but I wouldn't doubt it after all the things that have happened to you," he said, smiling calmly at me. Charlie wrapped his muscular arms around my shoulders leaning in. I could feel his warm breath on my face.

My face flushed from the anticipation of the goodbye kiss. He pressed his lips on mine. I gripped his arms in my hands and kissed him back. He slowly pulled back, "It was nice seeing you, Arielle."

"Same." Is all I could muster to say with a sheepish grin.

Charlie chuckled and released me. "Go visit Father Beau and let me know when you come this weekend. Oh, when did you find your Papa's book?"

"It's during the storm! Breeze was there. He helped guide me and you will never guess where the book was the whole time?"

"Egret's Nest?" he guessed with his palms in the air.

"Exactly. Things just get weirder and weirder."

"Funny how you keep going back to that place and you had never even noticed it before."

I agreed. "Yes, I know, that is odd."

"I have to get going. I would like to make it back and check on Aunt Nina's place today."

I ran my hand over his arm, "Okay, I'll let you go."

He gave me one more kiss and was on his way. I watched until he was out of sight. Okay Arielle, it is time to get things done! I told myself as I walked back into the house.

Mama greeted me by standing there pointing to the windows. "You said you would help me, and I can't do this by myself."

"Okay, let me get dressed and we will knock this out," I said going upstairs to change. It took us about two hours but we finished hauling all the boards and putting them away.

Maybe I should wait to visit Father Beau. Talking myself out of doing anything was very easy. *No, go today, stop delaying.* I fought my procrastination tendencies in my head. *After lunch, of course* I thought as my stomach growled at me.

"Mama, do you want me to make us some grilled cheese sandwiches for lunch?" I asked her as she was washing dust from the plywood off her hands.

"That would be so nice."

After lunch I lied to Mama, "I'm going to take a ride around town and see what happened. I'll be home before dark."

"Please be careful. There still might be branches down on the street or water. I hate you riding around on that motorcycle," Mama said.

"I know, I know," I said and thought to myself, *she has no idea that a branch in the road is nothing compared to the things I have experienced last year.*

I took a few minutes to write in my own book about what happened two nights ago during the hurricane.

… I was taken from my room and shown that a hurricane was not what I had seen before. Raging battles create the winds. Bloodshed is the rain. The clashing of swords creates the lightning. I wasn't hurt

80

even though I was in the midst of the battle. I saw a fire breathing dragon ignite a building on fire. CAT 3 is really Crusade Among Terrene level 4. Learn more about this!

I paused tapping the pencil on my lips thinking, *All the things I see on a daily basis and what might lie underneath. This room, this bed I am sitting on, is it all real? What is real? Maybe what I see is real and the experience last night wasn't real? I am now thinking too deeply and confusing myself.* I scribble a few more things finishing up the other night's events.

Turning to the next page, I let the words flow.

What is my new purpose?

Who will be my next mentor?

Who can I really trust?

Should I share more with Mama?

Why do the books keep getting stolen from me?

Should I maybe give all this up and hide in the swamps?

A shock flooded my hand causing me to drop my pencil on my book. Okay, I will take that as a no on the last question. The pencil floated and angled itself as if someone was holding it to write. The lead touched my page and struck through my last question.

Should I maybe give all this up and hide in the swamps?

Okay then, not an option! I grabbed the floating pencil and tried a new question.

Marry Charlie?

I waited and held the pencil. Nothing happened, making me smile at the possibilities. Okay, maybe these are questions I need to answer. Satisfied with my list I pushed the pencil into the small loop on the side of my book.

CHAPTER TEN

Father Beau

I bundled up for my motorcycle ride over to Father Beau's church. I carried my book and Papa's book in my bag with me. The storm left a lot of debris behind, so I had to be alert. Dodging the tree branches on the road I glanced around to check for power lines. There was some building that the winds tore off the whole side, leaving it exposed to the elements. The city surprisingly didn't have too much flooding. A few people stood outside their buildings with doors and windows wide open revealing they didn't have power yet.

The gravel crunched under the tires and the bike wobbled a little from the loose pieces, I steadied it and pulled on the black asphalt to park. I pulled my book out and read my recap of the events. I like to reread what I write to make sure I don't leave anything out. The unusual encounters echo a lot of the same things in Papa's book. We were both on very similar paths. I get it now, he was trying to let me be a kid for a long as possible, without the stress of having these gifts. I just wish he was here to guide me as things unfold. He was a fantastic dad and I miss him so much.

While I was leaning on the seat of the bike, the front door of the church swung wide grabbing my attention. There was no one in the doorway. Curious, I tucked the book back in my bag and stood up straight. "Hello?" I called toward the church. No answer.

Cautiously I walked toward the open door. The church bells began to ring from the bell tower. The sounds of "O Little Town of Bethlehem" chimed away. Lurking in the doorway, I peeked inside to see the dim lights of the candles flickering on the side alter. Stepping inside I glanced towards the left side of the church. Nope, no one over there either. "Hello? Father Beau? Ms. Marie? Is anyone here?" The bells finished their ringing. No sounds, not even birds chirping outside.

Maybe I should come back, I thought to myself. I spun on my heels to exit the still open doors when they slammed shut inches from my nose. Frantically pulling on the handles I could not get the doors to budge. What is going on? My eyes squeezed shut as I slowly turned back around. The candles flickered and one by one, row by row they extinguished. Smoke swirled in curly q's. The wispy swirls traveled together forming a grey shape. It flowed toward me and hovered about six feet above me. The grey misty smoke took the shape of a round headed creature with four arms, two legs, and two enormous wings. He didn't have any defined features since he was transparent. As he hovered, his large wings pulsed keeping him in place in the air. Small feathers of smoke drifted from his wings floating down next to me. I reached for it. Once my fingers connected with the smokey feather a bolt of lightning gave me a little jolt. The creature froze as its glare connected with my eyes.

"What?" I asked him with sass.

It opened its mouth and a flood of smoky feathers plummeted toward me. I raised my arms above me and created a blue bubble for protection. The agitated creature let out a screech moving to a different row of pews. It attempted three more blasts that were deflected from my bubble.

I kept on taunting it "Yeah, what do you think about that? You can't get me, can you?"

Stretching out its wings it bombarded the bubble with a stream of feathers. A small crack formed on my top left side. Attempting to repair the section, still the crack got bigger and bigger. Rounding my shoulders, putting my palms together, and focusing on the crack achieved nothing. A second crack appeared on the right side. The feather bolts continued attacking my bubble.

One of the feather's made it through the crack and shocked me. Why is this not working? Come on Arielle, you've done this before, do it again. Nothing was working. The cracks were turning into gaps in the bubble. The creature let out a war cry that was so loud my ears began to

84

ring. I couldn't fight off the feathers and the shocks became unbearable. Falling to my knees, I held my hand up trying to protect myself. Convulsing from the continuing shocks, I shook uncontrollably. My mouth was so dry. I couldn't hear or see and the pain was indescribable. *Help me!*

A man's voice sounded far away and said, "Arielle?" I felt a soft touch on my shoulder.

All I could do was groan, the pain was still lingering. The smell of burnt flesh filled my nose. Electric pulses ignited across my whole body in random places. I cried loudly when I felt arms under my shoulders and legs pulling me onto a flat surface. I tried to open my eyes to see what was happening, but the pain took over and I blacked out again.

Papa stood before me in a dark room, one spotlight directly over him showed he was dressed in his best Sunday suit. He looked at me with a tender smile not saying anything.

"Papa? Are you really there?"

The spotlight clicked off and we were in complete darkness. "Arielle, have you been still?" Papa asked.

"I think I have been, why are you asking me? Why can't I see you anymore?"

"If you have been still and know how to let your light shine, then you would know why your powers have failed you."

"They did fail me, why?" I asked Papa in the darkness. The light from a sunrise filled the area as far as I could see. Pulling myself to my feet I looked all around searching for Papa, but he was gone. I stood alone watching the brilliant colors of the sun develop on the horizon. It was the most spectacular sunrise I have ever seen. No boundaries, not a single obstacle to block the view or cast shadows, just pure light.

"Be still and let your light shine," Papa's voice echoed in my head.

"Why do y'all keep saying that, what does it mean, really? You want me to sit around doing nothing? You want me to be a flashlight?" I asked with too much attitude.

The silence was broken by a new sound. Beep, then the sunset disappeared into darkness for just a second. Beep, it repeated but this time the darkness took over the sunset longer. After about the tenth beep the sunset didn't return, and I was again alone in the darkness hearing a repetitive beeping sound. What is that sound? Where is it coming from? My eyes fluttered open and closed right away.

"Arielle?" a soft woman's voice asked.

"Mama?" I croaked.

I felt the warmth of her hand on mine as I managed to say, "Ouch." Very slowly. Her touch left my hand immediately. "I hurt."

"My precious girl. We are going to find who did this to you and they will pay for it," she cried.

Sleep took over and I was alone again in the darkness. The creature from the church cackled and hovered over me. "What do you want?" I screamed at him. I replayed the scene, my bubble was intact, but began to crack. Why couldn't I repair it? I know I have the powers to do this and I have done it before. What is different now? The tingle of pain jolted through my body. "Stop!" I yelled. The world went dark again.

My eyes tried to open again. I caught a glimpse that Mama was in the room with me sleeping in a chair. I squeaked out a whisper, "Mama?"

She sprung up and was bedside, "You are awake!"

"What happened? Where am I?" I whispered slowly.

"You are in the hospital, sweetie. Just try to get some rest, you are going to need to be still," she encouraged me.

"Be still?"

"Yes, your body was badly burnt, and you have bandages covering a lot of you until you can fully heal. They have some special ointment to try to save your skin."

"I don't understand. Is that why I smell burning?"

"Father Beau found you covered in burn marks right inside the church. No one knows who did this to you. Do you remember who it was?" Mama drilled me wanting answers.

"I don't know, but my body hurts."

"I will see if the nurse can give you something else for the pain," Mama said and quickly darted out of the room. Within seconds I was asleep again, waiting for the next visitor.

Be still? Well, this is a very harsh way to force me to be still, isn't it?

Aunt Nina's voice came to me, "Well my child, we have been telling you to be still, haven't we?"

"Yes, but this is a little extreme, don't you think?"

"This is not my doing. It is your own. You have been delivering messages to others for many years, and now you have your own message, but you decided you don't need to listen. God has other plans for you."

"You mean He did this to me? How could He? This is terrible, I'm in so much pain. Why'd He cause me so much pain?" I cried to Aunt Nina.

"Child, He didn't cause your pain, you did. If you would have done what was asked of you, then this wouldn't be your current path."

In my mind I crossed my arms in a huff, "I think this is pretty ridiculous."

"I think God feels the same way about you, do you really think he wants to see you suffer? Didn't He see enough suffering when He watched His own son die on the cross for you?"

"I didn't really think about it like that," I said in a lower volume.

"No, you didn't because you are too busy being loud. Be still child!" She exclaimed and was gone.

The beeping sounds returned, and I drifted away from Aunt Nina and back into the hospital room. With my eyes open I didn't call for Mama, I just laid there in my pain and attempted to be still. Following instructions is hard when they don't make sense. Be still Arielle, be still. Don't move, just breathe. Mama saw my eyes were blinking open and closed, "Can you hear me?" she asked.

"Yes, I can hear you."

"Do you need anything?"

"No Mama, I'm just trying to be still like you said."

"Good girl. I'm going to let the nurse know you are awake and seem to be doing okay."

CHAPTER ELEVEN

Road to Recovery

My discharge papers said "Be still." *You have got to be kidding me. This really has gone too far.* I thought to myself.

Charlie had come to visit. I wanted to run away with him and stay at his camp and never leave again. My arms and legs were badly scarred from the burns. I was grateful that my face was okay. On the short car ride home from Tulane Hospital, I ran my fingertips over the lines on my left arm that created a pucker where the skin tried to heal. The doctor told us the special ointment helped, but the damage was too deep. It was unlike any burn he had ever seen before, neither a chemical nor the sun has created these marks.

I repeated the conversation with the doctor in my head, my sarcasm seeped out, "Lucky me," I said out loud. I covered my mouth trying to put the words back in, but it was too late. Doctor Abney faded out of my mind. I gave Charlie a half smile without explaining my words. We sat in the backseat, and he placed his hand over one of my scars looking deeply into my eyes he declared, "You are more beautiful than the day I fell in love with you."

"I, I, I" Stammering, not sure what to say. This is the first time Charlie had said he loved me.

He pressed one finger over my lips, "Don't say anything, just be still." I fell quiet and he gently kissed me.

Mama cleared her throat as she pulled up to our home. Charlie helped me out of the car onto the sidewalk. "Do you want me to park the car and you can get Arielle inside?" Charlie asked Mama through the open driver's side window.

Swinging the door open, he got his answer. "Thank you, Charlie, you are such a dear!"

Mama got me settled on the couch and brought me a glass of iced tea, sweetened of course. We sat and waited for Charlie. Mama had been at the hospital every minute during my recovery. I saw Mark, Nicole, and Charlie as well, but Mama never left. I looked at her, the dark circles had taken over her eyes.

"Mama, go get some rest."

"I can't leave you."

"Charlie is coming soon, please go take care of yourself for a change."

"Okay, I could use a nap or an early bedtime." She chuckled a little deliriously. "Good night, I am so glad you are home and are going to be okay."

"I'm glad to be home too, Mama. Love you."

"Love you too, sweetie."

The front door opened as Mama took the first step up the staircase and she paused.

"Go to bed Mama," I commanded.

"Goodnight, Charlie," She called over her shoulder to him.

"Goodnight, Mama Kaye," he replied.

Charlie sat with me on the couch and brushed my hair gently away from my face. I turned to face him and said, "I told her to go to bed, she is so exhausted."

"Good idea. And now it is your turn. So, you can be still," he joked with me, tapping me once on the forehead.

"Y'all got my attention; I promise to be still."

I traced my fingers over the scars on my biceps. How could this happen to me? I have the power to beat these creatures. I've done it in the past. What has changed?

90

Charlie interrupted my thoughts, "Let me help you upstairs."

Charlie closed my door and went down to stay in Mark's room for the night. I cuddled up in my sheets. *It felt great to be home and in my own bed.*

My purse flooded the room with a soft purple light. I crawled to the foot of the bed and leaned over trying to reach it without stepping onto the cold floor in my bedroom. The strap was hanging on the back of a chair next to my desk. Stretching far I wiggled my fingers to touch the leather strap. "Come closer!" I commanded the bag. It levitated and fell on the floor. "That is not what I asked you to do!" I fussed at the bag. The color disappeared and the bag laid lifeless on the floor. Sitting with my legs crossed and arms crossed across my chest I scowled at the bag. "You can just stay there then. I am not going to pick you up." Out of spite the bag glowed purple, rose up and placed itself completely out of reach on my desk.

"That's not funny. Who do you think you are? I am more powerful than you, come to me now."

The bag opened and Papa's book flew out whizzing toward my head. I slouched down, barely getting out of the way. The book slammed against the white wicker headboard and landed open on my pillow. The pages frantically turned and paused.

My hands up as if I was under arrest I said, "Okay, Okay, maybe I'm not more powerful, but you don't need to try to hurt me. I've been through enough pain recently, wouldn't you agree?" The book stayed still, and a hint of purple lit up on the pages. I crawled to the head of the bed to see what was highlighted.

The words were etched in purple. As I read the words on the page, Papa's voice filled my head masking my own internal voice.

"Things are moving very fast now; my powers seem to be out of control. I don't know what has happened." The book flipped to the next page without me touching it. A few paragraphs down the letters glowed purple and I began to read again. Papa's voice was in my head as if he was reading his own words. "My world has changed, and my eyes are opened to more and more creatures. Some of them are more powerful than I am. I don't understand why I could defeat them before or why they are able to overtake me now."

I paused and sat straight up closing my eyes digesting what Papa was saying. It was way too close to what was happening to me now. Maybe Aunt Nina went through the same stuff too? Was this a rite of passage of some sort? I refocused on the pages of Papa's book to see where he wanted me to continue reading. I felt something wet press against the back of my arm. I cringed thinking about what it could be. What else could go wrong? As I turned my head to see I let out a sigh of relief.

"Breeze, I'm so happy to see you." Leaning to my right, I draped my arms around his neck, and he nuzzled close to me. "Thanks for being here." He gave my cheek a lick and pressed his fuzzy head on my arm. My hand landed on the book. He was pushing me to continue. "Okay, Breeze, I understand."

The book flipped a few more pages to reveal more information. "I had to learn that my powers were not mine. My life is not mine. I answer to God for all things. With a grateful heart I must remember to give all things back to Him. Let your light shine in a dark and fallen world."

"Breeze, I've lost sight just like Papa did, haven't I?" I asked.

He placed his paw on my thigh and let out a soft whimper.

"How could I be so stupid? It's so simple."

Breeze gave a side look with one ear cocked up and a slight grin as he swirled and evaporated into the darkness. He only came for short times, but I always when I needed him for guidance, just a little push in the right direction.

Be still and let your light shine. They were talking about me being humble. I have become so arrogant about my powers, that aren't even mine. I scooted off the bed and grabbed my own book and penned the words to record what I have learned. I hope to pass my book down to someone who could also learn from my mistakes. Hopefully, it won't take something so painful, and scar filled to learn it. The scars will serve as a reminder to keep myself in check. After I wrote all that had happened, I took three deep breaths, one for God, one for Jesus and one for the Holy Spirit and I prayed.

"Heavenly Father, please forgive me for losing sight that you're the Almighty. I can't do this without you or your guidance through the Holy Spirit. Will you guide me and mold me into what you want me to be? If I stray again, please push me in the right direction, maybe in a little less painful way. Thank you for the gifts you have given me. I promise to use them to do your will. Show me what you want me to do. Amen."

Snatched from my bed I was pulled up in a clear bubble-like tube through a hole in the ceiling. I shot out of the house traveling face first. My arms dangled by my sides and my cheeks became pink and fluttered from the force of the traveling. My nightgown danced around my ankles as I continued to glide at a great speed through the tube. A soft light glowed as the I came to the end of the tube gently placing on my bare feet, I could feel the soft, green mossy landing below me. The moss was warm under my feet and between my toes. I took a few steps looking in all directions. The stars filled the big night sky with nothing surrounding me. The landing was about the size of a 12-foot circle. Still alone I waited quietly sitting in the middle of the moss. My eyes began to feel heavy, so I laid down. The warmth of the sun on my face woke me. I was still in the moss. Resisting the urge to call out for help I decided to be quiet instead.

As time passed and the sun continued to rise and was not nearly directly overhead. My fair skin surprisingly didn't feel the normal burn which occurred after being out in full sun for more than twenty minutes. My tummy rumbled. *I am hungry, will you feed me?* I thought, looking up toward the sunlight for someone or something to provide something for me to eat. A cloud covered the sun creating temporary shade over me. A small white round disk popped out of the moss. I picked it up and took a bite. It tastes like bread with herbs. My stomach began to settle down after I had eaten the whole disk. *Thank you.* The clouds moved away from the sun revealing it was in the afternoon position in the sky. I stood and walked the perimeter of the mossy island. Looking down over the edge of the island there was nothing below.

Spending time alone is lonely. I settled back in the middle of the moss and sat with my eyes closed. *I am being still. I am listening. What do I do next?*

The sun began to dip down under the mossy island. *I am thirsty, will you give me something to drink?* A cloud appeared above me and rain poured down. My hair was plastered against my face, and I shivered from the coolness. Tilting my head back I pinched my nose and opened my mouth and filled it. Leaning forward again, I swallowed the mouth full of water. After about six refills, I wrapped my arms around me thinking, *thank you, please stop the rain.* The rain cloud stopped, and the moss sucked up all the extra rainwater giving me a dry place to sit again.

Stars began to twinkle in the dark sky. *How long will I have to stay here? What else am I supposed to be learning? Can I go home now?*

A lightning bolt shattered the night sky, breaking off into seven separate streaks. I cowered and laid flat against the moss. *Okay, I won't ask that again. So, I need to rely on you, ask you for guidance and all my needs? Thank you for providing for me, even when I don't act appreciative. Thank you for loving me. I am ready to listen, God.*

The moon slowly made its way above me. I laid on my back with my hands folded on my stomach, watching, and waiting.

The moon grew larger and brighter. The craters were perfectly visible. I reached my hand up toward the moon and extended my pointer finger to tap the moon. It flickered and fluttered. Although the moon did seem close, I was shocked I could touch it. I pulled myself up on my elbow to get even closer. My forehead was now touching it. Laying back down the moon engulfed my mossy island creating a snow globe effect around me.

Standing, I looked outside the moon seeing the stars around me evolve into colorful orbs of various sizes. The colors were all different. Soon there was no more darkness, just the soft glow of all the colors ever imagined in all different shades. The moon continued to move down through my island or maybe I was travelling up through the moon. Orbs overlapped filling the sky. Finally, I emerged on the other side of the moon among all the orbs. The colors circled around me creating a new bubble, I couldn't see outside of the orbs like I could when I was in the moon. I could feel the gentle motion as I began to drift with them, but not see our destination.

The weather changed leaving the air cooler. Rain tapped on the orbs as we continued to travel. I became sleepy, sat down and slowly drifted into a deep sleep nestled among the orbs. I stirred awake as I felt my surroundings changing. The orbs opened at the bottom and deposited me gently back on my bed. They floated above me and one by one they moved toward the window out into the night sky.

There was one left, it was a golden yellow color. I opened my palm and it landed there for about ten seconds before floating away and disappearing with the others that had gone before. I nestled back into my bed and tugged the covers up to my neck. I was tired but felt mentally rested from my pleasant journey. "Goodnight." I spoke into the night to whomever was listening to me.

The next morning, I recorded the events in my book and checked the date. Discovering I was gone only one evening I was glad I didn't have to explain to Mama where I was or what happened. I examined my scars and they had dramatically faded overnight. *Thank you for the healing last night, physically and mentally,* I thought, smiling at the ceiling. Stretching, I climbed out of bed to see what the day had in store for me. I still need to chat with Father Beau in hopes of locating Mr. Wolf and finding Aunt Nina's book.

CHAPTER TWELVE

Looking for Help

My goal was clear, find Aunt Nina's book and be humble about it. I felt it was good to start again. I dropped the gem I took from the Egret's Nest along with Papa's book and mine in my purse.

Charlie asked over breakfast, "Do you want company going to see Father Beau?"

I sipped my steaming coffee, "Maybe."

"I could go with you today. Tomorrow I might go back to the camp," he suggested.

"Perhaps." I wanted to clear my head and ask for some guidance and not get myself into the same pickle as before. Because of my injuries it had been almost a month since I last tried to find Mr. Wolf or talk to Father Beau.

"I'm not sure what you are thinking, but I really want to help you, Arielle," Charlie said with a bit of annoyance.

"I know. I'm just trying to figure out my course of action. Yes, if I do go, I would love the company."

"Thank you, that's a much better answer."

"You're welcome," I said smiling between sips of coffee.

Charlie reached out and ran his hand gently over my arm, "Your arms, they look so much clearer than they did yesterday. They changed almost overnight."

Smiling, I glanced at him as if to say, I'll tell you more later. "Yes, they do look better, don't they?"

Mama reached over and patted my other arm, "Arielle, they're healing so nicely! Keep doing whatever it is that you are doing."

"I will Mama. I'm going to sit outside for a bit," I said to them.

I found a sunny spot in the courtyard and centered myself. *Hi God, it is me Arielle, I could use a little guidance please. Can you show me where to go next? I think I need to find Mr. Wolf and get Aunt Nina's book back.* Concentrating on my breathing, I waited for an answer. My eyes glazed over as my mind opened.

Water poured into the courtyard filling the square where I sat. In the column of water, I saw Breeze cruise by, doggy paddling completely submerged in water. Random books floated by that I didn't recognize. Madame Fia appeared and drifted by on a bright green floating pool raft. A children's toy of three men in a tub bobbed up and down as it floated out of view. Even though I was under water, I could breathe normally. As the unusual items and people drifted by, no one contacted me or seemed to know I was there.

I sat alone in the water looking around. There was a white round plug with a silver ring in front of me. I looped my index finger in the ring and pulled upwards. The water swirling down the hole the white plug had covered created a suction sound. My world began to twirl around me in the water. The bench behind me floated up and rotated, the cement bird bath separated into two pieces and joined in the spin. Just as I got to my feet the water picked me up and I freely flowed with the courtyard items around and around as the water drained from the scenery. The hole in the ground grew and swallowed up the bench as it ended its spiral descent.

I realized I would be next to be captured in the drain. I couldn't grab onto anything to save myself. I tried to dig my heels into the water, but it just created a dip in the water panel making a "V" shape where my heels were. The swirling stopped and I entered the hole in the courtyard.

My free fall caused my stomach to drop. Curling inward I tried to contain my urge to vomit from the feeling. I hated roller coasters that made my stomach drop and this was just the same feeling. Slamming into a pool of water feet first I found that my shoes and clothes made it difficult to swim. The area was dark and cold, but there was enough light from the hole from which I fell to see walls surrounding me. *I must be in a swimming pool.* I frantically kicked and reached for the rung of a ladder. The water moved up and down with each item cannonballing into the water from the hole in the sky.

I pulled myself up the ladder one rung at a time trying to keep a good footing regardless of my waterlogged shoes. *What is the deal with unusual surroundings? I just want some guidance and I feel like I am living in a riddle instead.* I was able to find the top of the ladder. There was a circular wheel connected to a door on the ceiling where the ladder ended. Balancing myself I put both feet wide on the rung and grabbed a hold of the wheel pulling with all my might, but it didn't budge. I took a deep breath and tried again. It turned a bit with an iron groaning sound. Taking a moment, I regained strength and tired again, it moved a little more with a louder metal groan. On the third try the wheel clanked and a bolt came loose opening the doorway. Pushing the wheel up I climbed into the next room.

The room was dry and a warm yellow color with a single box in the middle of the room. A small bird hopped out of the box and perched on the edge. He was cobalt blue with an orange beak. He turned his head side to side examining me with each eyeball one at a time. His beady eyes watched me as I moved against the wall toward the left where a door was located. I whispered, "Hi little fella, I'm not going to hurt you, I'm just passing through." He squawked at me but didn't leave the box.

Slowly I reached for the door, the knob was very warm, indicating maybe fire on the other side. I gave the knob a twist and slowly pushed the door open about two inches so I could peek into the next room. The bird behind me began to screech loudly, so I glanced back to see what all the clamor was about. The bird had transformed into the same bird I saw last year numerous times. He was grey with four arms. Each time I had seen this bird trouble followed and was usually aimed directly at me!

I darted into the next room and slammed the door leaving the bird behind. His long talons clawed at the door. Quickly, I slid my back against the wall. A claw penetrated through the wooden door allowing the bird to pull a shard of wood away. He shoved his eye in the opening looking for me. In pure terror, I jabbed my finger directly in his eye. He screamed in pain and backed away. I took my chance and darted toward the middle of the room finding it was filled with red walls creating a maze. Sweat formed across my forehead, I used the back of my hand to try to remove some of it.

Stumbling through the maze my lips puckered from the heat. I began wishing I had some water to drink. I trudged on, trying to find my way out. *This was supposed to be a peaceful time of mediation, where did I go wrong? God, can you help me out here?*

Immediately the walls of the maze fell flat to the ground showing me the door to the next location. I climbed over the tumbled walls toward the door. The way some of them landed revealed about six walls teetering on top of each other. Finally, making it to the door I twisted the brass doorknob. This time I didn't peek, I went straight in and closed the door behind me. Soft sounds of a flute filled the room and the walls were a light teal color. It was very relaxing. *What is all of this and what am I supposed to learn from all these weird rooms?*

A deep voice silenced the flutes, "You have forgotten, to ask for help. You have forgotten why you asked for guidance."

I answered him, "I'm asking for help now."

"There's more to it than that. You need to once again find yourself and your way." The soft flutes played their melody.

I leaned against the wall absorbing the music. Closing my eyes, my mind drifted. Childhood memories flooded back. We were in Michigan visiting family. There was a dairy farm with black and white spotted cows. Yellow butterflies dance around a field with dandelions as far as the eye could see. I picked a dandelion and examined the fuzz in the perfect white circle. *I wish that I could find Aunt Nina's book.*

Blowing and twisting the stem in my fingers to catch all the white fuzz I did it in one long blow.

Aunt Nina's voice filled my head, "That's a great wish, but now you need to make it a reality, child."

"How? I still don't have any direction on where to go," I said to Aunt Nina's voice.

"Go back and see Father Beau, this time don't be so arrogant and ask for help if you need it," she warned with one clap her hands.

The room fractured and large pieces of the room broke off falling to the ground. As each piece fell the courtyard returned to my view. I was back home again. I stood in the courtyard looking for the plug in the ground, it didn't exist. The bench was in the right place as was the birdbath. I moved to sit on the bench when the side door of the house opened. Charlie came outside and sat next to me.

"Are you sure you don't want my help? I'll go with you to see Father Beau."

Aunt Nina's words echoed in my head. Ask for help if you need it. "Maybe it would be nice to have you come along."

"Nice? All I get is nice?" Charlie picked on me lightly pinching my shoulder.

"Okay, it would be stellar if you would come along with me. Is that better?" I joked back.

"I guess that will do. Are you ready to go now?"

"Yes, let me just grab my bag."

"I'll go get the jeep from the garage. Tell your Mama we are leaving."

I stood on the curb for only a minute before Charlie pulled up. I placed my bag containing the two books and other knick knacks on the floorboard. I pulled myself onto the worn brown leather seats.

Soon the crunch of the oyster shells under the tires indicated we were very close to Father Beau's church. Charlie parked the jeep and came around to open my door. Normally I would have pushed my way out and hustled to the church, but I was trying to be still and accept help. This was hard for me. Charlie flashed a smile. Charlie bowed down as he opened the door for me. We headed for the church.

As we approached the door, I thought to myself that Charlie's closeness made me feel a little better. The layout was different from the last time I was here. The fear of not having the power to protect myself was real. I still have not figured out how to combat this, but slowly things are being revealed to me. Apparently, I just must be still and be a flashlight.

We stood outside the large wooden door with ring shaped handles. Charlie said with concern, "You are breathing really hard, are you okay?"

"I guess I am," answering his question.

"Do you want me to open the door?" he asked.

"Yes, please."

He reached out his free hand to grip the ring and pull the door open. He stepped inside, but I didn't budge. Unlocking our arms, we naturally extended our arms and held hands as he looked around. The chapel was dark in contrast to the daylight outside. Charlie squinted as he looked at me and squeezed my hand, "Come on, we're good."

I cautiously followed him trusting his assessment of what he saw inside. There was no sign of the creature that destroyed me recently. But my palms were sweating from the fear and the memories that kept flashing in my mind. As we continued past the spot of my last encounter a jolt shot through me, and I gasped.

"Arielle?" Charlie stopped and turned to face me grabbing both my biceps "Are you okay?"

"Yes, just having a few bad memories," I whispered.

"Come on, let's find Father Beau." He pulled me along down the line of pews.

The stained-glass windows poured colors that danced on the altar as we briskly walked to the office. We made our way down the dark hallway as before. Charlie tapped on the door and called, "Father are you here?" He twisted the doorknob, pushed the door open and the dark hallway flooded with light from the office. "Who is here?" a woman's voice asked.

"Charlie and Arielle are here for Father Beau."

"Oh, please come in!" Ms. Marie exclaimed, "It is so nice to see you again." She rushed to the door and pulled us into the room. She wrapped her arms around me with warmth. "How are you? I heard about your encounter here at the church." She released me and ran her hands over my shoulders, then hugged me tight again.

"Hi Ms. Marie. I'm okay."

"Y'all are looking for Father. He's not here, but I would love to take a break and catch up. I have scones I could warm up in a jiff!"

Glancing at Charlie he shrugged leaving me to decide. "I would like that" I said trying to hide my disappointment that I would not be able to speak to Father Beau.

Ms. Marie pulled out an assortment of warm scones, a variety of teas, and hot water. "I needed a break from folding the bulletins for Sunday's service anyway," she said before taking a sip of her tea. "I know Father will be sad he missed you. He is out of town for a bit visiting family in Virginia."

"I really need to speak with him, when is he coming back?"

"It'll be a while, two weeks. I know you have not met our assisting Priest, but would you like to talk to him?"

"Um, well it's a sensitive matter, you know. About the things that happen to me. I'm not sure how comfortable I am sharing with someone that doesn't agree with my so-called gifts," I explained.

"I think Father Guidry is of the same mind frame as Father Beau. Would you like to just meet him?"

"I'll think about it. We really appreciate your time and the scones and tea of course."

"Well, you know you are always welcome here. I'm glad to lay eyes on you and know you are doing okay. Can I do anything for you?"

"Thank you, Ms. Marie. We will be back when Father returns. If you talk to him, let him know I need his guidance."

"Of course. God's blessings to you and Charlie." She squeezed me again before we left and patted Charlie on the arm gently. Asking one more time, "Are you sure you don't want to just have me introduce you to Father Guidry."

"Okay, but don't tell him anything personal please," I replied with pleading eyes.

"Oh dear, I would never! I'll be right back. Stay put and finish your scones." Ms. Marie bustled off leaving Charlie and I alone.

I glanced at him with concerned eyes.

"Arielle, you know Ms. Marie, she wouldn't do anything to put you in harm's way."

"You're right," I agreed with him.

Ms. Marie was gone for quite a while. "I can't seem to find him on the premises. I'm sorry to keep you waiting. I can tell you a little about him. He is from this area, a young fellow just a year out of seminary. He wanted to stay in Louisiana close to his roots. I haven't spoken to him about your gifts and I won't, but I feel like his soul would understand and like to help you on your journey too."

"We have taken enough of your time today Ms. Marie, thank you for everything. Please have Father Beau call me when he comes back into town."

"Absolutely, I will have him call you. Be safe child and I'll keep you in my prayers."

I was quiet on the ride back home. I didn't even realize we didn't take the normal route home. Charlie pulled the jeep onto a dirt road. "Where are we?" I asked Charlie.

"You need a little escape," he said. "I already talked to your Mama. She knows we are not coming back right away."

The road was lined on both sides with large oak trees. They loomed above creating a canopy over the road. He pulled up directly in front of the large plantation and put the jeep in park. There were no cars around as the sun was hanging above a large home with a wraparound porch.

I opened the door and slipped out before he could make it around to my side of the jeep. He blocked me from going any further. "Let's try this again." He pointed at the seat.

I sighed and climbed back into the jeep. He closed the door. I watched him as he straightened his t-shirt and pulled the door open for me with a slight bow again. I giggled at him, taking his hand he guided me out of the jeep. "Thank you, Charlie."

"You're welcome. And much better."

"Where are we?" I asked, looking around the large grounds.

"We're going to have dinner."

"Is this a plantation?"

"Yes."

"Do you know who lives here? How are we going to have dinner?" I asked pulling on his shirt sleeve trying to slow him down from walking up to someone's home.

"Do you have to ask this many questions?" he asked with a smirk. I followed him up the wide stairs to the wooden porch lined with rocking chairs. He reached for the elaborate door handle.

Grabbing his arm, "Charlie! You can't just barge into someone's home."

He gave a small chuckle pulling my hand off his arm and holding it tight in his hand. He swung the door open and we walked into the foyer. "Good evening," he called loudly.

"Master Charlie?" A man dressed in a black uniform greeted us in the foyer. "How lovely to see you. May I?" he said, extending his hand to me.

"May you what?" I asked. Turning to Charlie, "I don't understand."

"He wants to take your purse for you," Charlie explained to me.

"No." I pulled my bag closer. "No, I don't understand where we're. What is the place?" trying to clear up my confusion.

"Arielle, welcome to River Road Plantation. This is a very special place," Charlie said, extending his arms wide.

"What? I haven't heard of this place before" My eyes widened. I glanced around not blinking trying to take in everything.

"I'll leave you be," said the butler.

"Please wait, Arielle, this is Mr. Henry." Charlie introduced us.

Mr. Henry extended his hand. I quickly took it and shook it. "Nice to meet you, Mr. Henry."

"Likewise, Ms. Arielle." He made eye contact then turned to Charlie. "Will you be dining in and staying for the evening?"

"Yes, could you please prepare a room for each of us and let Mrs. LuLu know we will be staying for meals."

"Right away Master Charlie," he said and bustled away.

"Wow, I want to know everything about this place." I gazed at him waiting for him to spill.

"Come on, let me show you around the grounds while they prepare the house." He said taking my hand.

Charlie led me on a winding path with beautiful foliage and some late blooming flowers. The plantation was lightly decorated for the Mardi Gras season that was just about to begin. Purple, green and gold color sheer cloths were draped on the pergola in the garden. The sun started to dip down behind the tree line along the back of the home. A little chill blew through causing me to shiver. Charlie put his arm around me. "So, River Road Plantation is a place I have visited a lot with Aunt Nina. After my parents died and I was living with my uncle, she would take me over the summers and occasional weekends to get away." He paused and gazed at the trees that surrounded us then continued, "There is magic here. The people who visit and live here are like you. They have powers of all different kinds. I hope you can find comfort while we are here." Charlie said, facing me and looking directly into my eyes.

"Thank you for bringing me here, Charlie." I said, locking eyes, "I cherish moments like this and you sharing with me." I leaned in and he wrapped his warm arms around me.

"Let's go in and see what's for dinner," he suggested.

"Sounds good to me."

The table was set for two, one at the head of the table and one to the right. The other eighteen chairs remained without table settings in front of them. The chandelier sparkled above the center of the custom, ornate dinner table. There were real candles lighting the room giving a very warm romantic feeling. Charlie pulled my chair out and motioned for me to sit. He gave a gentle push moving my chair in with me. He sat and pulled his napkin out and placed it in his lap. I followed his lead.

"Charlie, this is way too much," I said leaning over to him, so the workers didn't hear me.

"Relax and enjoy yourself," he smiled tenderly at me.

"I'll try."

A man came and filled out water glasses then returned with a bottle of wine showing it to Charlie.

"White or red?" Charlie asked me.

"No clue. Something sweet?" I guessed.

"How about we try a Moscato tonight?" Charlie requested.

The man nodded and came back showing him a new bottle. Charlie agreed, "Good choice." A small pour was placed in Charlie's wine glass. He swirled it taking a deep sniff then sipped. The man and I both watched for his approval. "Fantastic," Charlie remarked with a thumbs up, "I think you will love it."

"I like it and it's sweet just like me," I joked with him.

He gave me a small chuckle and held out his glass for a full pour. "Thank you," he said appreciatively.

The six-course meal was paraded out and placed in front of us. The wine filled our glasses several times. My cheeks were getting flushed, and my giggles became more and more frequent even when things were not very funny.

Charlie placed his hand over mine before dessert arrived and said, "It's so nice to see you laugh."

"I couldn't agree more. Thank you, Charlie, this has been awesome," I giggled, raising my glass toward the ceiling spilling a little on my shoulder. "Oops."

Charlie gingerly took the glass from my hand smiling at me not saying a word.

"I guess you're right. I've had a little too much," I said with a huge hiccup at the end of my sentence. "Why are you so wonderful?" I said, placing my chin in the palms of my hands with elbows resting on the table staring at him."

"God made me this way."

"Yes, He did. Good job, God," I said, gazing upwards and giving the ceiling a thumbs up.

CHAPTER THIRTEEN

Night of Terror

Waking up in the large room was unfamiliar. Lightning flashed outside the floor to ceiling windows. The deep purple velvet drapes pooled on the floor that hung from the crown molded ceiling. I gently ran my hand over the soft curtain looking out toward the large oak trees that lined the drive. The full moon peeked out from the rolling clouds and cast some light on the scenery, but each flash of lighting helped me see clearer.

A figure was coming down the drive. I couldn't tell if it was a man or a woman, but it was walking like a human. There were others following behind. I moved away from the window not sure if I was dreaming or awake. I peeked out again and two eyes glowed red right off the porch. It was Mr. Wolf. Questions raced through my mind. *How did he find me? More importantly, why is he here?*

Sitting on the plush bench at the foot of the bed I quickly tied my shoes. My bag glowed. I found the gem was shining bright and was cool to the touch. I placed it in my pocket for safe keeping. A high screech echoed by the window, I opted not go back and look. Instead, I opened the bedroom door slowly trying to keep any creaks to a minimum. I didn't want Charlie to know I was going outside to confront Mr. Wolf. He had done enough for me. Swiftly and silently, I crept down the long hallway to the main staircase and slowly descended. The foyer lit up with a flash of lightning casting shadows around the rooms.

Glancing at the windows in the grand room off the left of the foyer I could see figures outside. The inside of the home gave me comfort, but I knew now that walls cannot always keep me safe. The spirits, demons, and even angels moved freely. Walls could not keep them at bay. I didn't look for any symbols posted on this plantation home to see what type of dwelling this could be. Creeping to the front door I pressed my face to the beveled glass panel. Keeping my eyes wide I waited for the next large flash of light to show me what I was up against.

The boom of the thunder was accompanied with a long flash. Hundreds of creatures gathered on the ground outside the front of the home. I started to panic. *I can't do this alone.*

Something brushed against my leg causing me to let out a loud, "Gasp." Jumping back to see what was in the house, my body relaxed in relief. "Breeze! I am so glad to see you." I knelt next to him and nuzzled my forehead into his thick white fur. "What am I going to do?" I asked him, locking our eyes. He licked my cheek with his cool wet pink tongue. "Stop that," I giggled. "That doesn't answer my question." I sat next to him and wrapped my arms around his neck listening to the thunder, howls and screeches as creatures gathered outside the plantation.

Closing my eyes, I prayed. *God, are you there? I know I have not asked for much help lately. I guess I have forgotten how much I need you. How could I be so stupid? Could you send angels to assist me in what is about to happen?*

Breeze gave a soft whimper and evaporated from my arms. My eyes fluttered open. Lifting my head, I rose from the floor. I opened my palms along my side and tested out my powers. A few zig zags of blue light sputtered out. *Come on, please I need help!* I shook my hands, placing them back at my side, palms up.

"Here we go," I said standing firmly in front of the foyer door. The door opened and separated from the house before floating into the night sky. The walls began to unlock from each other just like had happened at my house. The walls peeled away behind me leaving me floating on two wood planks like skis. Stepping off the wood the entire home snapped out of my view into a different realm of time. It disappeared like the sunset on the horizon in fast forward. I was alone facing the creatures in front of me.

Okay God, I really could use you now! I know I am not alone; I trust you. Show me what to do and please protect me.

I held my stance with my palms open, two small blue bubbles formed, one in each of my hands. The clouds parted and the full moon appeared, casting light on us below. Standing on his two hind legs Mr. Wolf approached me curling his lips showing his pointed teeth as he snarled. Still wearing his hat perched between his tall ears his body was covered in wolf hair puffing out around his tight, zipped vest. I could see his long full tail swaying behind him, but I couldn't see his legs or feet under his full jeans and dark boots.

Looking up at him looming over me, I shouted at him, "What do you want from me?"

"You'll open this book for me," he commanded, holding Aunt Nina's book in his overly hairy human hand. The book began to glow a pink color. It gave a shock, making him drop it. It flumped on the dirt ground. He growled shooting eyes like daggers at me. Bending down, he retrieved the book and held it tightly.

"I don't even know how to open her book so good luck with that," I said folding my arms.

"There's always a way to bypass the lock. Your Papa was on to something before he died. Your powers are greater than you think, but you are too green to even know what to do with them," he sneered.

"Don't you ever talk about my Papa again! I refuse to help you. Why don't you return the book back to me and I'll let you go unharmed?"

"You think I would agree to that dumb suggestion? I know you don't have it in you to battle us," he said, waving his arm showcasing all the creatures around him. "I saw what happened to you at the church."

My brow furrowed in anger as I realized that he saw that. Fear started to creep in with doubt. Maybe I am too naive for these great powers. I can't control them. Breaking my thought, something wrapped around my left arm above my elbow. I snapped my head around to see what it was.

The squeeze on my arm increased. I slapped it with the blue bubble that was still in my palm. I incinerated the tentacle, burning it in half, releasing my arm. There was a deep red mark left behind. The light of the moon remained glowing as I glared at Mr. Wolf. "You are going to pay for that."

"Child you are so oblivious. You keep talking like you know what you are doing, the only person you are fooling is yourself," he responded to my threat.

The rainstorm had moved on, but the winds picked up moving his fur plastering it flat against his face. The moon shone bright, helping me to see. Sounds swirled around my ears, *Arielle you are not alone. I am not alone?* I asked the words to myself then saying, "I am not alone! "I am not alone Mr. Wolf."

"You don't have anyone here," he scoffed, opening his arms wide showcasing only his posse. The creatures cackled at me.

The gem in my pocket floated out and away from us. The gem spun creating winds swirling a small tunnel in the sky. The point of the tunnel spun around and touched down between Mr. Wolf and me. The funnel morphed into a tube and filled with a blinding white light. I shielded my eyes keeping my blue bubbles toward the light source.

A booming voice came from the spinning light. "She is not alone." My face broke into a hopeful smile. Keeping my focus on the light, a random bolt popped out of the spinning tunnel. Following the bolt, a trail of light followed like a comet. The bolt circled around me and gently landed to my right forming a shape. He was about nine feet tall with soft white glowing curls cupping his human-like face. His broad shoulders held a magnificent set of golden wings. They arched up about three feet taller than him and draped down touching the ground. He wore dark brown leather armor around the trunk of his body. His arms were muscular and toned. He rested his right arm on the handle of a sword that was an electric blue color. He smiled gently at me as his battle scar across his left cheek disappeared out of my view.

I whispered, asking, "Jacob?"

"Yes. Hello Arielle, you are never alone," he answered in a smooth voice.

A long howl interrupted us, I wanted to ask Jacob, my assigned angel, so many questions, but it would have to wait.

Mr. Wolf charged us, signaling to his gang to attack with a wave of his arm as he tucked Aunt Nina's book inside his vest. Jacob took flight circling our battlefield. I stood firm and used my blue bubble to pulse out shocks on the creatures closing in on me. They each had their own powers or tools to fight back. Bobbing and weaving from their attacks I focused on what was right in front of me. Jacob was targeting others helping me defeat them. I didn't see Mr. Wolf but concentrated on the bird I was currently battling. Each blue bubble scorched off a bundle of feathers, causing him to fall unable to rise. He shot a few long flames out of his beak. My bubble blocked and extinguished them. The bird retreated, but I knew he was still out there regaining his strength. A transparent red round cage came rolling out of nowhere gobbling me up. I tried to grab a hold of the frame and shake loose. I couldn't escape from the cage.

"Jacob!" I called. He was far away in the sky battling other flying creatures. "Jacob! I need you! Help me!" My voice fell flat among the battle cries.

Mr. Wolf approached me circling the cage, "You really think you and your little guardian could defeat me?"

I rotated in a circle keeping my face toward him as he moved around me like I was his prey. "This isn't over," I told him.

"What are you going to do now little girl?" he taunted me.

I lifted my lit palms aiming at him. He gave a puff in my direction and both palms went dark. Looking at my hand I shook them to regenerate them. A few sparks came out, but they would not light up again.

"I'll ask you again, what are you going to do now little girl?" he laughed loudly.

My heart fluttered and a moment of fear caught me. *What am I going to do?*

Mr. Wolf raised his hand up sending the cage and me airborne. He pointed with his index finger, commanding a long-woven rope to attach to the cage. Turning, he walked, pulling me along with the rope wrapped in his hand like a child with a giant balloon.

I frantically looked around screaming, "Jacob! Jacob!" He was so far away now he couldn't hear me at all.

Mr. Wolf pulled me down the River Road, leaving behind the beautiful oak trees and the battle. Reaching the end of the trees, he opened his free hand and made a circle motion in front of us. Turning back to look at me, he chuckled. A large hole opened in the sky. He stepped inside the area beneath the hole pulling me behind him.

"Wait, stop, maybe we can work something out," I pleaded with him.

"Too late," he said as he looked into the next world we were about to enter. He tugged hard on the rope. The cage bumped into the side of the hole. I lost my balance falling.

My eyes widened in fear seeing the next realm. Flames blasted from the ground and screams of terror echoed all around. On my knees I grabbed the cage again, rattling it trying to break free. Mr. Wolf pulled again to adjust the cage to clear the hole. The cage wouldn't budge. A flash of white caught my peripheral vision. Blinking rapidly, I spun around searching for the anchor. Jacob had his hand wrapped around the flat bar holding me to keep me from bouncing with Mr. Wolf. I held my tongue. I didn't want Mr. Wolf to know that Jacob was here. He kept tugging on the rope finally looking back to see how the cage was stuck. He realized that Jacob was the reason the cage would not move.

"Let go Jacob, she's mine now."

"She isn't alone, and I'm not letting her go with you," Jacob responded with deep fury.

"You're not powerful enough to defeat me, Jacob. You know that." Mr. Wolf pointed out.

"I'll call her other angels."

Mr. Wolf curled his lip over his teeth, "I'll get her into my realm before they can help her. Do you really want to attempt this?" he cautioned Jacob.

Jacob held tight to the cage. The winds between the two worlds picked up causing his locks of hair to swirl around his face. He pulsed his wings pulling the cage back toward the oak trees. The forceful wind he produced whipped the air around us. I climbed toward Jacob, putting my arms out of the square holes in the cage I held onto Jacob's arms Between the two of us a light formed. "Let your light shine, Arielle," Jacob told me.

Voices filled my head as I focused on small white circles appearing before me. Papa said "Arielle, you're a strong woman and I believe in you." The white light began to grow as I listened to Papa. I truly believed in his words.

Aunt Nina's voice came next. "Sweet child you are learning so much, remember what I was able to teach you, use what you know to continue to grow. You can defeat anything or anyone. Keep God's white light with you at all times," she encouraged me.

I focused on the light between Jacob and myself as it grew larger. It began to melt the cage creating a small opening.

Mr. Wolf growled, "You're coming with me." He pulled forcefully on the cage.

I lost my grip and fell flat onto the bottom of the cage. As I fell a white bolt of light came from my torso enlarging the area of the cage that was now open. My ears rang with a high-pitched sound as I watched Jacob continue to pump his wings, keeping me from being pulled-into Mr. Wolf's world.

Scrambling to my feet he put his right arm inside the cage, and I held on with both arms extending them straight along with my legs dangling. Letting go of the cage he reached in with his left arm. I squinted hard putting my face in his strong chest as he wrapped both arms around me, he spread his wings wide as we pushed away.

Mr. Wolf yanked the cage into his realm, but I had already slipped out. I wrapped my arms around Jacob's neck as he held me in his arms. We watched as the red cage was sucked up into the other world. Mr. Wolf howled in anger. I could see him whip the cage around behind him facing out looking at us. He smiled mischievously, reaching into his vest to reveal he still had Aunt Nina's book in his clutches. "This isn't over yet!"

CHAPTER FOURTEEN

L is for...

The hole began to quiver, and large chunks fractured and disappeared revealing the world we were still in. The creatures that accompanied Mr. Wolf retreated without their leader. Their purpose began to fade. Jacob held me until Mr. Wolf was completely gone. He swiftly glided us back to the plantation door. Placing me on the ground he waited for me to get my bearings.

He lifted my head with his glowing finger under my chin. "You are getting the hang of this, just remember you are not alone, you don't have to do this alone. Call on God and He will deliver you. Let your light shine Arielle, it is a very dark world we live in, even if you can't see the darkness around you," Jacob told me.

"Now what?" I asked.

"Call on me and I'll appear as long as you have the gem," he assured me. "God will provide for you. Be still and listen to Him."

"I know I really got off His path, didn't I?"

"You have free will to choose your own path. I'm here as your guardian to protect you when you ask for it."

"Thank you for being there for me. I'll be calling again soon, I'm sure!"

"I was with you the night of Crusade Among Terrene as well because you had the gem with you."

"So, I have another item to keep up with?" I tried to joke with Jacob.

"Just try not to get sucked into another world. It isn't always easy to get back," he warned.

We stood in total darkness, "Where are we?"

"There's a transition place between worlds. We're in between Mr. Wolf's world and yours."

"Are we stuck here? Is it hard to get back home?" I asked Jacob.

"I can go anywhere I'm called. It's a little harder for you to move between actual worlds, but the transition is not as tricky."

"Well, how do I get back to Charlie now?"

"Ask for it to appear to you." Jacob said as he lifted himself into the air with his mighty wings. "You already have the power, just find the path."

I watched him fly away into the night like a fading star. "Okay, appear to me." I said with a shoulder shrug. Nothing happened. I stood alone with the moon shining on me and the line of dim Oak trees swaying in the light breeze. I took three deep breaths. Lifting my face to the stars and moon. I asked again, but with more conviction, "Reveal to me the world where I should be."

Deep purple clouds rolled in covering the moon and stars, small pinhole beams of light poured out of the sky. Light twinkled like fireworks and they filtered down to the ground. The rushing wind filled my ears so I could hear nothing else. As I watched the lights dance before me in the sky, a sense of peace washed over me.

I prayed, *Thank you God for delivering me home, Thank you for sending Jacob to protect me. Please help me keep you the center of my world so I always know what you want me to do to honor You and all Your glory. Amen.*

The winds abruptly stopped. My ears opened to the sounds of the crickets chirping and the trees rustling in the wind. I dropped my gaze and saw the plantation. Everyone inside was asleep, missing all the excitement. I walked quietly back to the front door, opening it slowly trying to not wake anyone. Removing the gem from my pocket, I gently slipped it back in my purse. At least I now know how to call on Jacob.

119

The bed was so inviting, I kicked off my shoes and curled up under the covers. Slumber took over and I fell into a deep sleep.

A soft tapping sound woke me. "Yes," I said with the croaking voice of the morning.

"Arielle, do you want to come out for breakfast?" Charlie asked without opening the door.

"You can come in, Charlie."

He opened the door "You doing okay?" he asked.

"Yes, I just need you to come hold me for a bit," I said, pulling the quilt back inviting him to the bed.

Standing over my bed he plucked a long white feather from my hair and examined it, "I guess you had a bit of an adventure last night?"

"This must be Jacob's," I said taking the feather back and placing in gently on the nightstand, "Will you just hold me for a bit?"

He sat on the edge of the bed and untied his brown work boots, pulled them off, and let them clunk on the hardwood floors. He swung his legs into the bed and wrapped his warm arms around me.

I sighed and relaxed in his embrace. "Charlie?"

"Yes, Arielle."

"What would I do without you?" I asked him.

"I guess you would have a boring life?" he joked, tapping my nose with his finger.

I laughed and rolled back to face him, "Yeah, how'd you suppose that?"

"You would have never met Aunt Nina. You would have never gotten to come to this plantation home either. See very boring life. Come on, are you ready to get some breakfast?" he encouraged me to get out of bed.

"Yes, I'm hungry, but so tired."

He kissed the top of my head then my cheek. Sitting up in the bed he slipped his feet back into his boots lacing them up. "The coffee's ready, see you in a bit."

"Okay, I'm coming."

He closed the door and I laid there for a minute thinking about how much my life had changed since these powers evolved. I used to just give strangers messages from loved ones. I do miss that part of it and wonder why I wasn't getting those messages anymore. My life had become complicated and unknown. A mere two years back I wasn't battling creatures. Things were unraveling way too fast now.

After breakfast Charlie suggested we take a walk around the grounds. "I kind of did that last night," I joked.

"You want to tell me about it?" he asked, grasping my hand as we walked.

"I'd like to just enjoy the world around us right now."

He nodded, swinging my arm gently.

A red cardinal followed us as we walked down a path to the gardens that lead to a wooded area behind the plantation. The cardinal peeped at us and flew along the path ahead. The soft rustle of the leaves and the crunch of the twigs under our feet reminded us of how far away from the hustle and bustle of the city we were.

Charlie stopped and sat on the wooden bench; he patted the seat next to him for me to sit. I did and wrapped my arm around his waist placing my head on his shoulder. "Can we just stay here forever?" I asked.

"No, this is not our place in life, but you can always come visit anytime you want. Speaking of your place, I called your Mama and let her know you were here so she wouldn't worry."

I smiled up at him, "Thank you for taking care of me." My heart took over as the words fell out of my mouth, "I love you, Charlie." Wide eyed I slapped my hand over my mouth not realizing the words escaped.

Charlie turned pulling my hand away from my mouth he gently grasped my chin turning my face toward his. He placed his warm full lips on mine, our eyes instinctively closed. As he pulled back, he whispered, "I know."

Air blew out my nose in a small laugh.

"I love you too, Arielle," He said seriously this time.

"So, can we just stay here forever now?" I said in a playful tone with my shoulders pulled to my ears trying to make myself adorable with batting eyes.

"Not a chance, but we can stay a few more nights. Do you plan on going back to talk to Father Guidry?" he asked.

"I think I should wait for Father Beau. What do you think?"

"I wish I knew what advice to give you, but really, you know much more than I do about who you should keep in your circle."

"That's so not true! You suggested your Aunt Nina and she was the right person I needed. I really could use her now," I said with my eyes welling up.

Charlie tapped his finger over his top lip thinking hard while resting his thumb and middle finger under his chin. He glanced to the side searching for something in his mind.

My tears dried up watching Charlie think so intensely, "Charlie?" I broke this thought.

"Let's head back. Do you want to play some corn hole or horseshoes?" he suggested.

122

"No. I want to know what is going on in your head," I said, pulling away from him, resting my hand on my neck with my elbow toward the sky.

"I have to figure some stuff out, but you know I will share with you. I always do," he said, pulling my hand away from my neck trying to calm me a little.

"Fair enough," I said with a little eye roll, but secretly excited to play corn hole.

He stood holding the bean bag close to his chin with one eye closed. He focused on the hole on the wooden board. Stepping forward he tossed the bag. It slapped on the board and slid perfectly in the hole dropping into the grass below.

I slapped my thigh as I stooped down to pick up my corn filled bag. I tossed it up in the air catching it. I bounced it twice in my palm lining up my toe with the hole I swung back and released my bag perfectly.

I jumped in the air pointing at Charlie, "Oh yeah, winning point right there!"

He laughed at my excitement. "Okay, okay. Why don't you go inside for a bit? I have a few things I need to work on while I am here."

"Is there anything I can do?" I asked.

"Why don't you find Ms. LuLu, she might have something for you."

"Alright. Where?"

"Try the kitchen first, or maybe in the veggie garden?" Charlie suggested pointing toward the back side of the home off to the left.

CHAPTER FIFTEEN

Ms. LuLu

"Ms. Lulu?" I called from the foyer as I closed the front door.

Walking into the kitchen I asked again, "Ms. LuLu, are you in here?" A few pink and purple bubbles appeared and popped outside the kitchen window. Peering out, I could see a round woman bending over in the garden. She wore a denim dress with a white and blue apron. In the crook of her arm, she held a wooden basket that was flat on the bottom. She stood up and pointed in the basket counting what she had collected. She sauntered down the path between the tomatoes and out of my view.

Finding a side door, I took the four short steps down and walked a well-worn dirt path to the garden. The closer I got I lost sight of the lady in the garden. A few more pink and purple bubbles appeared and popped in front of me. "Hello? Ms. LuLu are you out here?" I asked into the bushes.

The tall bushes shuffled as a buttery voice replied, "Yes." Her head appeared between the leaves as she parted them with her small brown hands. She flashed a bright white smile against her smooth brown skin. Small dark freckles moved as her checks rounded from her smile and her eyes twinkled. "Oh, I was hopeful we would get to chat."

"Have we met before? You feel very familiar," I asked the face peeking through the leaves on the tomato plants.

"No, but I see your soul and it feels familiar to me as well. I was watching you last night with your angel. What is his name?" she asked.

"Oh, how did you see me? I thought I was not here," I asked with my brow scrunched up in concern.

"Ms. LuLu sees a lot that others do not," she said, referring to herself in the third person.

My lips squeezed together creating a thin line, as I thought about what I should say next.

"Are you going to share with me his name?" she asked again.

"Oh yes, sorry. His name is Jacob."

"What a perfect name, Jacob," she smiled through the plants.

"What do you mean?"

"Jacob means to go behind or follow. Sounds like God has him following you," she explained.

"Or maybe going behind me to help me with the messes I get into?" I suggested.

"Possibly that too," she chuckled. She gave a little flick of her index finger and thumb at me creating little purple and pink bubbles that floated over toward me. They landed on my nose. The smell of roses and lavender filled my nostrils. I closed my eyes and took a deep breath. My mind wandered as I was transported to a field of flowers. Rows of lavender, tulips and rose bushes as far as my eyes could see. The warm sunlight dusted my cheeks as I walked, running my fingers along the tops of the lavender bushes.

I heard a soft pop of a bubble and was back looking only at the darkness of my eyelids. Fluttering my eyes, I could see the small bubble was gone and Ms. LuLu was still there smiling at me through the tomato bushes.

"What just happened?" I asked her softly.

"You experience my gift. This is what I can share. What's your gift?" she said, flicking a few more bubbles off down her garden path.

"I used to give messages to the living from those who have passed on, but I haven't felt that sensation in a while. I have powers to protect myself and others, but lately I have made a mess of things."

"That can happen from time to time, have you spent time being still and centering yourself?"

"I guess not. I'm trying, sort of," I said looking down at the dirt I was moving around with my shoe. "I was kind of getting guidance from Aunt Nina, but... now that she is gone, I'm taking a break I guess."

"Sweet girl, you don't take breaks from this kind of gift. This world needs your gifts all the time. Can you imagine how many people you didn't deliver a message to? They are missing that bit of peace that you can deliver to them."

"I guess you are right. I don't know how to turn it back on."

Ms. LuLu changed the subject, "Would you like to help me pick some vegetables for dinner?"

"Um, sure, but how do I get to you?"

"You have to go back to the beginning and make your way here," she pointed back toward the house.

I trotted down the path through the tall bushes. Picked the next aisle over and made my way back toward her. "Ms. LuLu?" I called when I was about where I left her.

"I'm over here," she was about 2 rows over now.

"I thought you'd wait for me."

"Try again. Come four rows over next time. Things aren't always what they seem when you're in the middle of them."

I repeated my steps and came back up the aisle, "Ms. LuLu? I'm back."

"Here I am," she waved the branch of a bush to get my attention.

"Oh good, I picked the right row this time. What am I looking for?" I asked.

"First, realize that the path you are on doesn't define you. You can always go back to the beginning to end up where you need to be," she said in a soft voice.

"Yes Ma'am." I nodded in understanding.

She lifted a purple eggplant showing it to me, "This one is a good size and the birds have not gotten to it yet." She took the top of the eggplant in her hand, holding it tight, snapping the stem and placing it in her basket. "You pick the next one."

I folded back the leaves looking on the stalk for a similar size eggplant. "How about this one?" I asked holding the base of the vegetable for her to see.

"Look at all the sides."

Looking closely, I examined all sides. "It looks good to me."

"Okay, pick it and we will cook it up for dinner."

"What are you making tonight?"

"We are having eggplant parmesan."

"Do you want help in the kitchen tonight?" I asked Ms. LuLu.

"Sure, I will never turn down help. Do you turn down help?"

I knew she wasn't talking about kitchen help, "Well, I'm a little stubborn," I admitted.

"Don't let your pride get in the way of the path you should be on."

"I'm trying." I said with a bit of annoyance. *She doesn't know what I have been through, she doesn't know my struggles and that I must depend on myself.*

"Let's get cleaned up and start working," LuLu suggested and strolled back down the row toward the house Down the path she would randomly flick pink and purple bubbles at the plants.

"Why do you do that?" I asked.

"No reason, other than to keep my gifts sharp."

"So, no one is seeing what you are putting out there?"

"Nope," she continued to flick out a few more bubbles. "But I know the plants like it."

As we entered the kitchen she pointed to the sink, "Wash up first."

As the water heated, I noticed a small blue jar with a pump. I lathered the soap playing with the suds. Ms. LuLu flicked a few bubbles in the mix. I giggled at the colors it created squeezing them with my palms they popped and new bubbles populated.

My hand projected a small translucent arch. The interior of the arch appeared as a film strip. It slowly began running the reel. There was a small girl spinning in a circle giggling. She spun enough to make herself fall. Landing in a pile of autumn leaves, she picked them up and tossed them in the air letting them drift down to earth.

She was having a ball all by herself. Along the tree line a silhouette of an animal appeared. It crept closer; I saw it was a wolf. He came closer so I could see he was wearing the same hat that Mr. Wolf was wearing in each of my encounters.

I called to the girl, "Watch out! Pay attention!"

She couldn't hear me and was playing in her own world. Mr. Wolf was not in a human form, but full wolf. The little girl picked up her head and called, "I'm coming." Then she ran off into the house. She dusted the leaves from the front of her dress. The leaves continued to fall from her as she scampered up the short stairs to her light blue house. The wolf sneered in my direction and darted off back to the trees.

My hands became cold and I snapped back to reality. The warm water had run out of the faucet.

Ms. LuLu asked me, "You're hands clean yet?"

"Oh yes ma'am," I said, twisting the knobs to off.

She handed me a linen towel to dry. "See anything interesting?" she asked.

"I really don't know yet."

She smiled and pointed to the eggplant, "Let's start here first." She washed her hands quickly and dried them on her fresh apron.

Then she rinsed the eggplant and placed them on the butcher block She handed me a knife. "Cut here." Using her finger, she showed me the size of the eggplant slices she wanted. Once the eggplant was sliced, she spread them out and lifted her hand high in the air, twisting her index finger and thumb and she released salt to fall on the flat eggplant. Repeating this several times, she nodded and dusted her hands on her apron.

What else is in her index finger? I asked myself.

She clapped her hands and indicating the tomatoes. "Rinse these please."

As I returned them to butcher block, she asked, "Did you cook much with your Mama?"

"Sometimes. I would watch her in the kitchen a lot when she would cook for us and all the foster kids we had in our home."

"That's a lovely memory," she smiled at me warmly, "Next we're going to make a red sauce from scratch," she explained.

I nodded waiting for my next instructions.

"Use the same knife to dice these and put them in this pot."

I worked on my task as she cut up fresh onions, celery and green bell peppers that she had collected from the garden. We tossed everything in the pot. Ms. LuLu clicked on the gas burner under the pot and gave the items a quick stir with her wooden spoon tapping it three times on the thick metal pot.

"Let's check the eggplant." She pointed to the slices, "See the sweat?"

I nodded, "Why does it do that?"

"The salt pulls out the extra moisture, so your meal isn't too soggy. Can you flip them and do the same with the salt to the other side?"

"Sure." I mimicked her salting of the eggplant, but no salt released from my index finger, so I grabbed the shaker instead.

"Good job. Check the pot and give it a stir."

I nodded and did as she told me. I had my back to the kitchen as I stirred glancing in the pot from time to time. I felt an arm around my waist. I jumped, dropping the wooden spoon in the pot as Charlie whispered in my ear. "You look like you know what you are doing."

"You made me drop my spoon!"

He laughed, releasing me. "I see you found Ms. LuLu."

"Yes, I did," I said, glancing over at her. "You didn't tell me she was so... special."

"Everyone at this plantation is special to me," he responded.

I gave him a side glance, not sure what he was trying to tell me. I let it go and figured I would ask him in private. "You coming to help us?" I asked him instead.

"Nope. This is woman's work," he joked.

Ms. LuLu hopped up from her wooden stool and snapped the kitchen towel at him, "Git!" she fussed, "Go do some man stuff then," she joked back at him.

He chuckled, "Okay, I'll go cut some lumber." He exited.

I watched him go and smiled softly, shaking my head.

"That boy is a mess, ain't he?" Ms. LuLu wanted me to agree.

"He is, but he's my kind of mess." I turned and smiled at her before fishing my spoon out of the pot then rinsing it off. I kept stirring to keep the red sauce from sticking to the bottom.

"Y'all do have a very beautiful connection." She flicked a set of pink and purple bubbles. I felt them land and pop on the top of my head.

My vision changed and I saw the world through her eyes. She replayed the scene she just saw of us in the kitchen. Charlie gave Ms. LuLu a shush motion with his index finger in front of his puckered lips, not making a sound as he slipped his arm around my waist.

I watched our faces through her eyes. I saw the love between us. I also saw I needed a haircut! From the back my hair had lost its shape and was just hanging. I know that was not the point, but it was still something to consider! The bubbles popped and I was back in the kitchen and began stirring the pot.

"You're really good at sharing your gifts, aren't you?" I remarked to Ms. LuLu.

"Lots of practice. Here let's add a few spices." She sprinkled from a variety of jars into the pot, "Keep stirring."

"How much longer till it's ready?"

"Soon. Can you pat the eggplant dry with a fresh linen and then make a single layer in the baking dish?"

She then added breadcrumbs over the eggplant then the red sauce over my layer. She handed me the bowl containing large shards of fresh parmesan cheese. I laid them over the red sauce and slipped one in my mouth to eat when she wasn't looking.

"Repeat the layers again then we are ready to bake." After I finished, she slid the pan into the oven. "Go freshen up, dinner will be ready in about 30 minutes," she said waving her kitchen towel at me.

Charlie was sitting on the porch out front. I closed the front door and sat next to him on the matching rocking chair. "Dinner will be ready in about 30 minutes."

He reached out his open hand and I took it in mine as we rocked in unison. He smiled asking, "You wanted to ask me something in the kitchen?"

"Uh yeah. So, what do you mean everyone is special to you here? I need some explaining."

"I'm not trying to be cryptic, everyone is special to me, but they all have their own special gifts that are normal or supernatural too."

"Why didn't you tell me?" I asked, trying to pull my hand away in annoyance.

Charlie held tight not allowing me, "You have to understand everyone here may not want to take the time to start over teaching someone, I wanted it to be their choice. Ms. LuLu seemed to take notice of you as soon as you came here."

"Why wouldn't someone want to help me? I'm not troublesome."

"Arielle, most everyone here has lived their life giving their gifts to the best of their abilities and are looking for a place to wind down if that makes sense."

"I guess so, but Ms. LuLu said, 'You must use your gifts to help others. That is why we were given them' or something like that. She seems nice, how many others here are like her?"

"Really most of the staff is special to some degree."

"How did they manage to get everyone in one place?"

"This plantation has a calling. I don't know how they know to come here, but when they do, they always remain. My lineage was the first to settle here. Ms. LuLu has known me all my life. She doesn't have the same knowledge as Aunt Nina did, but maybe she can give you a little push back to where you need to be," Charlie suggested.

"Thank you, Charlie." I stood and gently sat in his lap draping my legs over the arm of the rocking chair. Resting my head in his neck I asked, "You sure we can't just stay here forever?"

His voice vibrated on my forehead, "I wish we could, but there are bigger things for you."

The front door opened, and Ms. LuLu called to us, "Come and get it while it's hot."

Charlie and I took our seats at the long table. My head cocked to the side examining all the extra food thinking to myself, this is way more than Ms. LuLu and I had prepared this afternoon. I nodded as I took a bite of the eggplant, proud of what I helped create tonight.

"You did good," Charlie told me, patting my hand gently.

"Thanks, but you know it was all Ms. LuLu," I admitted.

LuLu flicked a few bubbles at the table as we continued to enjoy dinner. They landed in Charlie's wine glass. I could see her from where I was sitting, her shoulders bounced from her giggles in the doorway. She disappeared back into the kitchen leaving us all alone. I watched, waiting for him to drink. He sipped the water. Encouraging him to take a sip I lifted my wine glass to toast, "To a wonderful few days at River Road Plantation."

Reaching for his wine glass he halted and glanced in the glass seeing the bubbles, "You two are up to no good, aren't you?" He lifted it once and sipped anyway.

I watched him still holding my glass hopeful to see what he was seeing, but I didn't. He shook his locks and blinked a few times coming back to the room.

I sipped the wine and asked, "What did you see?"

His brow showed deep wrinkles of concern, "A wolf."

I almost dropped my glass, but quickly set it down. "What did he want?"

"You."

Ms. LuLu was back in the doorway, her joyful personality had changed to a face of worry.

"What do I have to do?" I asked Charlie, but half asking Ms. LuLu, who was not moving.

Charlie put his hand over mine, "I don't know, but we can figure it out."

"I need to get Aunt Nina's book back. That is what he wants me for, to open it, but I don't know how."

Ms. LuLu cleared her throat.

"Yes, Ms. LuLu what can you add to this?" Charlie said, inviting her into the room. He motioned for her to sit across the table from me.

She pushed the elaborate flower arrangement away from us so she could see my face. "I have her key, sort of," she said.

"How'd you have it?" I asked, a little more surprised than I should have been.

"Aunt Nina and I go back longer than before you were even thought about."

I nodded. realizing I wouldn't have been the only one she mentored, or came into contact with special gifts. "What is it?"

"It's very unique and you will have to travel into the swamps to get it."

"You said you had the key, sort of. What does that mean?" I asked Ms. LuLu.

"I used to have the key, but you can always acquire another one."

"What is it?" I asked again.

"Of course, my dear, sorry about that. It's the tooth from an albino alligator."

My mouth twitched to the side trying to figure out how to accomplish this. "Well, I had the book, but it was stolen from me by Mr. Wolf. I don't know his real name, but he's part wolf. He wants me to open it. Now I need to find an albino alligator tooth."

"Sounds like we are in a bit of a pickle. You need to get that book back and I'm sure Charlie can help you with the alligator tooth."

"Any suggestions on how to get it back?"

"Charlie told me Mr. Wolf is looking for you. Let him come and take the book back from him."

"That's what I tried to do when he was here last night. Did you see everything?"

"No, all I could see is what happened on this side of the oak trees. Once you ventured beyond, I lost sight of you."

"Well, I don't quite remember where I was when what happened, but Mr. Wolf captured me in a cage and was trying to bring me into another dimension or world. Jacob was able to rescue me, thank goodness, I couldn't do it by myself. We were totally outnumbered too."

"We can be prepared for the next time he comes."

"Do we just wait for him to come? Can we get him to come when we want him to?"

"That isn't something I can do, but maybe someone else can," Ms. LuLu said, looking at Charlie.

"Not me, I don't have any powers, you know that, Ms. LuLu, but I can take you to get that tooth," Charlie said, holding his hand up like he was under arrest.

"Charlie, I know you have something special in you. You just don't believe."

"Nope, I'm gifted with the ability to connect people to each other, that is my gift. And get you close to an alligator," he said, convincing himself with a hard nod and a chuckle.

"Do you want to at least try to explore it?" Ms. LuLu asked in a soft sugary voice.

"What about Mr. Jacques the groundskeeper or Ms. Adeline the maid?" Charlie suggested trying to push the focus away from him, "Heck, Arielle might be able to since he is looking for her!"

I just watched wide eyed wondering if Charlie did have some kind of powers or gifts? What a duo we could make! What if our kids would have the same powers or even better ones? My mind wandered, kids… Ethan, my nephew, showed some signs of seeing creatures when I was visiting him last. Maybe I am not as special as I thought; everyone seemed to have powers.

"Arielle?" Charlie called me back, "Did Ms. LuLu give you a bubble?" he joked.

136

"No, I was just thinking," I said shyly, not wanting to share my daydream.

"Obviously, but did you come up with anything?"

"I don't think I did, my nephew came to mind, and I realized that there are a lot of us with these so-called special gifts, so maybe I am not so special," I said in a sobering voice.

"You don't have time to feel sorry for yourself, we're all special in some way or another. Each of us are God's chosen children, once you know what he wants from you then you can really blossom," Ms. LuLu advised me as gently as she could.

I nodded, "I'm not sure about how to contact him."

Charlie perked up, "What about Father Beau? He should return in a few days. Why don't you go home and pack some things and we can go find that alligator tooth? I'm sure my cousin Nick can help too. Then we will go meet with him after all of this."

Ms. LuLu smiled, reminiscing, "Father Beau is such a nice man, that one is."

"In the meantime, why don't you meet the rest of the staff before we head out tomorrow," Charlie suggested.

"Sounds like a good plan," I agreed. After dinner Charlie took me to meet Mr. Jacques, Ms. Adeline and the rest of the staff who lived at the plantation permanently. Everyone was very welcoming. I look forward to coming back and spending time with each of them and getting to know them better.

CHAPTER SIXTEEN

Gator Tooth

I packed the rest of my items in a duffle bag. Mama ran up and handed me a tube of sunscreen lotion. "You might need this, even though it's winter, you know you burn."

"I have a hat Mama, I'm okay."

She took my hand and examined my arms where the burn marks were, "You're looking better, but I want you to be safe. Take the sunscreen," she said, putting it in my hand.

I unzipped my bag and stuffed the tube in. I patted the bag and said to her, "Got it."

She hugged me, "Don't be gone too long, I want to spend some time with you before I go to Michigan. Are you sure you can't come with me?"

Releasing her I said, "Mama I have already been through this with you. I'm not going. I'll go next time. I promise."

She sighed and gently placed her hand on my arms giving them a squeeze. "I'm going to miss you."

"I'll miss you too Mama, I'll be back with either alligator or fish for us to eat."

Charlie tapped on the front door asking, "Arielle, you ready to head out?"

I pointed to the duffle bag, "Yes, I'm all packed. I was just telling Mama we will come back with some kind of seafood."

"Yes Ma'am, we will!"

Charlie picked up my bag and put it in his jeep. He opened the door and I jumped in waving to Mama through the open window. "Bye, love you."

"Love you too, sweetie."

As we rumbled away, I asked Charlie, "Will Nick be taking us on his fishing charter?"

"That's the plan. We'll go out very early tomorrow. He has seen one albino alligator in the swamps. It has been a few weeks since the last spotting."

"I can't get over that he has actually seen one. Other than the one at the zoo I didn't know they were real."

"Unfortunately, they don't last long in the wild, being all white it's hard for them to camouflage themselves and poachers get them," Charlie explained.

"I'm looking forward to seeing his boat and catching some fish too."

The next morning Charlie woke me up before the sun, "Arielle, we really need to get going," he said, shaking me gently.

"Oh no, it's way too early," I complained.

"Coffee is on the boat and I'm leaving in 15 minutes," he warned.

I flung the covers back, "I'm up, I'm up!"

The chilly morning air cut through my jacket as I tried to warm up by taking small sips of coffee. We arrived quickly at his cousin's Nick camp. I had not been to his place before. The sun was barely peeking over the horizon highlighting his camp with a pink hue. Charlie tied his boat to the pier offering me his hand to balance and join him. We walked up the old wooden stairs to join Nick who was waiting on his porch.

"Morning cuz!" Charlie said reaching for his hand. They slapped hands and did one firm shake.

"Mornin' ready to find da gator?" Nick asked in his thick bayou accent.

"Ready," Charlie said.

We boarded Nick's boat, which was much larger than Charlie's. He has poles, hooks, fishing gear, a spear and a machete. I looked at Charlie and secretly pointed to the machete with a questioning look. Charlie shook his head as if to say, don't ask, because you don't want to know. I gave him a sheepish grin and found a seat toward the front of the boat.

The motor clicked into gear as the boat backed away from the slip. Nick swung the boat around and we were heading out in seconds. Nick asked me over the loud motor, "Ya been gator huntin' before?"

"Hunting?" I asked.

"Yes um, huntin'."

"Well, no, I thought we were just getting a tooth not the whole alligator," I confessed.

"How ya reckon you get that single tooth, sha?" Nick pointed out.

I glanced at Charlie and back at Nick. "I don't want to kill the albino alligator. I just need a tooth."

Nick looked toward Charlie, "I'll let you handle this." and he turned forward to steer the boat.

"Arielle," Charlie started gently, "You understand we are going to kill the alligator to get the tooth. Right?"

"But isn't there another way?" I pleaded. "They're rare, and doesn't this make us just like one of the poachers?"

"No, because we will eat the meat and use all the parts. It will just happen to be a rare alligator," Charlie explained as best he could.

"I don't like this. There has to be another way."

140

"I'm open for suggestions," Charlie said.

"What if we sedate him and pull a tooth?"

"If we sedate him, where do we put him to keep him safe until he wakes up?" Charlie asked.

"In the boat? On the shore?"

"Let's think about this logically. In the boat how smart is that?" Charlie quizzed.

"Not so smart." I confessed.

"On the shore that is marsh, how will we get him on the shore and ourselves back in the boat without getting stuck in the marsh?"

"If we had my little pirogue we could try."

"I don't think you realize this is about a 15-foot alligator, he'll not fit in your small boat."

I sat quietly thinking, but no logical ideas came to mind. Nick cruised in and out of areas for hours. The sun was high above us. "We may well go home for lunch and try back later," Nick said, turning the boat.

We spent the afternoon searching for the alligator with no luck. "T'morrow is another day." Nick offered up, "Same time?"

Charlie replied, "We'll be here in the morning. Thanks for taking us out today."

"It's been fun y'all maybe we will have better luck t'morrow."

Charlie and I putted home in his boat for the evening. The next day didn't produce any different results and neither did the next one. "Maybe we should just try again another week?" I suggested to Nick on our way back in for the night.

"Your call, Sha" he said. "I'm free till Saturday."

"I really need to go back and spend some time with Mama before she goes to Michigan."

"Na same time t'morrow," Nick suggested as he pulled the boat into the slip and cut the engine.

I looked at Charlie for validation. He smiled and said, "I'm game for whatever."

Nick said, "It's settled. See y'all in the morning."

I complained to Charlie over dinner, "I have to get up early again! I am not cut out for this."

He chuckled, "Arielle, you're way too much sometimes."

"What does that mean?" I said, turning my tone a little too annoyed.

"Calm down, I'm just playing with you."

"Sorry, I am not used to all the early morning activities. I think I'm a little extra cranky," I admitted.

"I know." Charlie said with a smirk trying to make light of the situation.

"If we can just get that tooth, I can get back to sleeping in," I laughed, changing my mood.

"Tomorrow. I have a good feeling," Charlie said.

The morning started out the same as usual, early and cold. Nick started toward the normal spots where he had seen the alligator. Going on the third hour we rounded the bend on the small water way when the sunlight danced off a stark white leather body. Nick cut the engine and the boat dipped forward to a slow glide. Charlie took the fishing rod near him and tapped the water, Wap, wap, wap. I held my breath and watched. Nick moved with grace to the front of the boat and hurled a few marshmallows as far as he could throw them. They plopped softly in the water with perfect ringlets around the impact area.

142

The sounds and smells got the alligator's attention. He slithered into the water heading for the marshmallows to investigate. His white snout popped up and gobbled both puffy treats in one chomp. Nick and Charlie both giggled like schoolgirls. "Don't kill him," I whispered to Charlie. "I have an idea."

"Now you got an idea," Nick said quietly and slightly annoyed.

"What if I can stun him with magic and we can tow him back to Charlies? Then you can keep him as part of the alligator farm," I shrugged.

"Huh, that might just work," Charlie said.

"Magic?" Nick asked with a scoff.

"Will you let me try?" I asked.

Nick opened his palm and said, "Go right ahead. Dis your show anyway."

I looked at Charlie for reassurance. He nodded and said in a whisper, "Go ahead."

I folded my hands and closed my eyes to say a little prayer in my head. *Dear Father, you already know the outcome of this adventure. I am asking you to give me the power and the wisdom to not harm this alligator. Amen.*

"Okay, get your net and ropes ready I'm going to stun him," I instructed the guys.

We all stood close with our eyes on the gator. "Maybe we could be a little closer?" I asked.

"Naw, da boat will scare him," Nick said.

"But what if you can't reach him with the net and he drowns?" I asked.

Charlie shook out his net making it flow, "Arielle, where is your faith?"

I waved my hand slowly and took a larger stance focusing on the gator. I could see his white snout and eyes on the surface of the murky swamp water. The cool breeze caused the Spanish moss draping in the cypress trees to billow. The sun sparkled on the dark water. I took a deep breath and smiled. I gave myself a little pep talk, Okay Mr. Alligator, I am not trying to hurt you, and you will be safer with Charlie.

Placing my palms together I opened my fingers wide and created a small blue bubble.

"Woah!" Nick said as his eyes got wide watching me instead of the alligator.

"Get ready," I said positioning my bubble to line up with where I think the body of the alligator would be under the water. I let out the blast toward the gator. It made contact and the huge reptile flung its body around in a rolling motion.

Charlie and Nick tossed their nets over the gator enclosing him. He wasn't stunned and tried to pull free from the nets. Charlie hollered, "Hit him again!"

I press out another blast and as the white body sank into the dark waters, the guys pulled the nets toward the boat with the gator wrapped inside. They took care to make sure his head was above water as they repositioned him as best they could in the nets. He was about 12 feet long. "He is alive, right?" I asked the guys.

"Yep, he is breathing. Do we want to get this tooth now in case he wakes up?" Charlie asked, clicking his pilers.

"Sho 'nuff. Den release him if he wakes," Nick agreed.

"What can I do?" I asked the guys.

"If he wakes up, blast him again," Charlie said.

"Got it." I stood aiming at the limp gator hanging over the side of the boat wrapped in nets to make sure I didn't accidently get one of the guys.

Nick opened the mouth of the alligator as Charlie leaned over with the pliers saying, "I guess anyone will do." Charlie fastened the pliers around a small one of the bottom teeth and pulled up with all his might. A deep groan came from the alligator.

"Is he waking up?" I asked.

"No, but that must have hurt," Charlie said.

"What y'all reckon we do now? Let 'em go?" Nick asked.

"I think you should keep him, so he is protected at your alligator farm," I said to Charlie.

"We do have him caught. I have an empty pen we can keep him in until we figure out if he is a she or not," Charlie convinced himself.

We toted the alligator back to Charlie's camp and got him maneuvered into a small enclosure without any issues. Charlie took the tooth from his jean's pocket and placed it in the palm of my hand. "Ask and you shall receive," he told me.

"By golly what in the sam hill is dat back there?" Nick directed his question to me.

"I have a gift of sorts that is still a work in progress," I told him.

"Charlie, why you no tell me about dis stuff with Arielle?" He asked in a hurt tone.

"It isn't my story to tell," Charlie said.

"Thank you for all your help, Nick. I hope to be able to repay you one day."

"Sha, book you a fishing charter" he suggested. "But leave dat magic at home."

I laughed with a wink and a thumbs up, "You got it."

"Now that you have your tooth, you can spend the next week with your Mama before she goes to Michigan," Charlie said. "Why don't you give her a call?"

CHAPTER SEVENTEEN

Mama to Michigan

While spending the rest of week with Mama, we chatted about her upcoming trip back to Michigan to visit family. She wanted me to come with her, but I had other plans. I crafted a believable story as to why I couldn't go. She still didn't know everything that was going on and I wanted to keep her safe and out of the loop as much as possible.

She sighed and said, "I understand Dixie is having a rough time, I know she needs you as a friend," Mama said believing my story.

Dixie was my best friend. I could use her anytime as a decoy since she knew all that had happened to me and had experienced some things firsthand with me. My battle last year on Halloween was an eye opener for both of us. She was with me as my gifts unfolded and I learned to communicate with the dead and pass messages on to the living. As I am learning about my new powers, I continue to face many challenges. Luckily, Dixie was someone I could talk to, but she wasn't able to help guide me, that is where Aunt Nina came into play.

Aunt Nina knew how to teach me to protect myself and fight. I tapped my necklace thinking about her. It was one of the enchanted items that she helped me create to ward off evil spirits. She also made me a quilted vest for protection. I still wear the necklace every day, but this only helps keep minor spirits from attempting to come near me. I have learned there are different levels of demons, and I am not able to always project myself as I learned earlier at the church. During that encounter I wasn't wearing the vest, but I don't think it would have helped. For Mama, keeping her in the dark was the best way for me to keep her safe. The less she knows, the better. Even though she knows there are some unusual things going on, I still want to try to protect her.

I figured I should go spend some time with Dixie in case Mama follows up with her or checks in to find me while she is out of town for the next month or so. Coming down the stairs with my helmet in hand I called out, "Mama I am going to Dixie's I will be back later. If Charlie calls, will you let him know?"

"I sure will," she called from the kitchen, "You be careful on that bike, people are driving crazy out there."

"Yes, Mama."

****

"Hi, Ms. DeeDee," I said, swinging my leg off the bike and placing my helmet on the handlebars.

"Hello Arielle. Dixie isn't here yet. She is having lunch with Ernie," she told me, patting the chair next to her, "Have a seat."

"Okay," I said, latching the gate behind me and taking a seat next to her on their porch, "How long ago did they leave?" I asked.

"She should be back soon, they left a few hours ago. How are things going with you and your Mama?"

"Good, Mama's planning her trip to Michigan."

"Oh, how nice. Will you be joining her this year? I heard your family really missed seeing you last time."

Thinking quickly, not realizing I would have to come up with a good excuse. "I wanted to stay here and spend some time with Dixie." It seems like Mama and Ms. DeeDee had been talking. Watching her face as she poured a glass of lemon water for me, I looked for her expressions showing that she believed me.

"Oh, I see," she said with her pencil thin eyebrows arching. The sliced lemons swirled around the top of the glass pitcher and a few plopped into the glass.

"Thank you," I said smiling.

"Seems like Dixie is doing very well," she said pointing with her glass toward the sidewalk. Dixie and Ernie came strolling up, walking hand in hand with smiles a mile long across their faces.

This might be harder than I thought, I said to myself. I stood up waving at them and called, "Hey Dixie, hey Ernie."

"Hey Arielle, I didn't know you were coming over," Dixie quipped.

"Yeah, I had some things I wanted to talk to you about." I said, bouncing my eyebrows to indicate I wanted some privacy.

"Sure," she said slowly and turned to whisper to Ernie. She giggled and they kissed goodbye.

"Bye, Arielle." Ernie waved to me, "Goodbye, Ms. DeeDee." Then waved to her and started his walk home.

"Byeee," Ms. DeeDee and I sang in unison.

"Come on, let's go inside." Dixie motioned to follow her.

In her room I sat on the plush carpet floor and she sat next to me. "What's up?" she asked immediately.

"Okay short version, I told Mama you were having trouble and I didn't want to leave you to go to Michigan. I need to buy some time to figure out some things going on like how to get Aunt Nina's book back. I'm onto something but need time. Can you cover for me?"

"Sure, but you know my Mom and your Mama do talk," she reminded me.

"Yeah, I gathered that from our little conversation waiting for you. You can figure it out right? Just say you have a few hiccups with Ernie."

"Sure, but what about you not actually being here to help me since you are here to help me? You know my mom is gonna tell your mom you are not here."

"Um, how about this? Say Charlie is in town and I'm here," I said pointing to the floor. "If your mom asks 'Where is she? Why haven't I seen Arielle?' Say I have been leaving before she gets up and come back after she is in bed in order to spend time with Charlie," I suggested with a slight shrug.

"Okay, I don't buy it, but I will try to sell it," she laughed.

"I'll stop by as much as I can to make it believable. We can make it like I am spending the night here."

"Alright, since we are talking, I have something to tell you," Her face beamed, waiting to spill everything she had been holding inside.

"Oh man, should I be scared?" I joked.

"Yes, well no, I mean maybe?" she said, biting her bottom lip waiting for me to reply.

"Really? Spill it!"

"Will you be my maid of honor?" she squealed!

"Holy crap, holy crap. For real? Like he proposed? Where's the ring?" I said grabbing her hand.

"He picked it out, and it's on layaway. So, I don't have it yet, but he proposed today at lunch."

"No ring. No deal. I'll say yes when I see a ring on your finger," I said wagging my left hand in front of her.

She slapped my hand lightly, "For real, I'm serious, this is happening. After everything that happened to me, well us, at Halloween. My eyes have been opened wide. I'm not waiting for life to happen. I need to embrace it and make it happen. We're getting married and starting a life."

150

"What about your school? Your dream to change children's lives as a teacher?"

"I can have that too. I'll finish school," she wrung her hands and examined them, not looking me in the eye anymore.

"Wait a minute, what are you not telling me?"

"Oh Arielle, why do you have to be like that?"

"Like what? I know you better than anyone else, you are not telling me everything."

She just stared at me.

"Wait. Are you? … Are you pregnant?" I exclaimed.

"Shhh!" she exclaimed, pushing her hands over my mouth looking back at the closed door.

"No! No! Are you?"

"Stop it, be quiet," she whispered to me.

"Are you?" I asked again in a whisper this time.

"Maybe?" She said with a half-smile.

"Maybe? You either are or you aren't. Which is it? You can't possibly be maybe pregnant."

"Okay, yes. I haven't told anyone, except Ernie of course. He's over the moon and so am I."

"You're the last person I expected this from. You wanted to finish college and become a teacher."

"I do and I will. Aren't you happy for me?" Little tears formed in the corners of her eyes.

"Yes. I am. I'm just a little shocked. When will you tell your mom?" My face tilted to the left and I continued. "Wait this is perfect, all the more reason I need to stay here, right?"

"Seriously, you are making this about you now?" Dixie shook her head in disbelief.

"I'm sorry, but really it does make perfect sense when it all comes out," I joked trying to make light of the situation.

"You never answered me," Dixie pouted.

"Absolutely, I'll be your maid of honor, can I be the Godmother too?" I beamed.

"We'll see," she joked.

"That's just rude!" I laughed back at her, "Okay anything else earth shattering you want to drop on me?

"Nope, I think I have dropped everything possible."

"Let me know when you tell your mom, so I can steer clear for about a week."

"You're just full of jokes, aren't you? Hey, I might need you for backup that week. It would work out well for you and your little plot to get out of going to Michigan."

"So true. Keep me posted. I love you, Dixie and I support you in all your life endeavors. You know that, right?"

"I love you too, Arielle."

A quick hug and I was off again to see if Charlie had called.

As soon as I got home Mama caught me and said she was catching a flight out next week, "There's no way I can talk you into going right?"

"Mama I can't tell you what is going on, but I really need to be here. I'm sure you will find out soon enough."

152

She gave me a side glance, "Okay, but I'm going to be checking up on you. Sending your brother here to spy on you."

"Okay, Mama, but I may be at Dixie's or Charlie's for some of the time."

"You better call and check in wherever you go."

"I promise I will, hey, did Charlie call?" I asked, changing the subject abruptly.

"No, he didn't."

The rest of the week passed slowly. I spent a little bit of time with Dixie asking if she told her parents yet and she hadn't.

Finally, Mama had her bags packed at the front door waiting for the taxi to arrive to drive her to the airport. "I really wish you were going with me. Aunt Mabel really wanted to see you. She has a large button collection she wants you to see. Your Aunt has been collecting for a decade now. The jewelry she makes with them is quite amazing. I'll get you something and bring it back as a treat for you."

"Thank you, Mama, and that sounds so tempting. I'm sorry I won't make it. I'll go the next time, I promise." I had other pressing things on my mind than a family reunion. A mission to get Aunt Nina's book back and take down Mr. Wolf.

Mama wrapped her arms around me, pulling me close, holding me tight, but gently. "I'm going to miss you." The soft perfume, L'air de Temps, filled my nose.

I closed my eyes and held her back with my head resting on her shoulder. "Me too, Mama, I love you." The sounds of a double honk outside our home made me lift my head and look toward the front door, "I guess your ride is here."

"Yep." She released me and grabbed the smaller bag.

I took the heavy one and followed her outside pausing to look for the driver. He was leaning against the car with arms folding looking down. My heart dropped seeing the man, he wore the same hat as Mr. Wolf. Pausing at the threshold, I squinted, examining him to determine if it was Mr. Wolf or not. Mama tugged on her suitcase to pull it over the brick sidewalk. Glancing over at her I saw the wheel had gotten caught and the case tumbled over, "Oh drat!"

The taxi driver was quick on his feet helping her pick up the case and move it to the trunk of the bright yellow car with black checker pattern down the side.

"Thank you very much," Mama told him. As I just stood there with the other bag trying to catch a glimpse of his face. Mama quickly came back and took the handle from me and rolled the suitcase over to him. I slowly followed her moving my head left and right still trying to see his face as he plopped the suitcase in the trunk.

"Arielle?" Mama called from the back seat of the cab.

"Yes." I said in a short tone. I was still trying to make out the driver's face that was now blocked by the lid of the trunk. The driver never looked up at me, pushed down on the trunk, the hinges made metal creaking sounds and the latch clicked loudly, securing the trunk. He turned and walked to the driver's side. He slipped in and shut looking forward with his black leather gloved hands resting on the wheel. He waited for Mama to get settled in the backseat.

Mama got out of the backseat and stood with her door open resting her arm on the top of the cab. She waited for me to respond. I left the curb and walked around the front of the car to the driver. Mama stood on her tiptoes to look over the hood of the car at me, "Arielle, what in the world are you doing?" she called to me.

"Just a minute Mama," I said, holding up my index finger to shush her. "Hey!" I called to the driver. He sat with both hands clamped on the black steering wheel looking forward and down a little so I still

154

couldn't see his face clearly. I wrapped my knuckle on the window and repeated, "Hey!"

He snapped his head up and turned to face me. I jumped back, stumbling into the other lane of traffic. Luckily, no one was driving around us. "Mr. Wolf!" I darted back at the cab and flung the driver door open.

The cab driver yelled, "What the hell lady?"

My face was level with him, it was a chubby rounded pink face under the hat, not Mr. Wolf. "Oh!" I said in shock.

"What is your problem?" He fussed at me.

"I, I, I" I stuttered shifting my weight and moving back away from him, "I thought you were someone else." My face wrinkled in confusion.

"Arielle, what is going on? I need to catch a flight. Are you okay? Should I stay?" she asked over the roof of the cab.

"No Mama, I'm fine. You're right, you should go. I was just confused." I turned my face to hers and walked over to her side. The cab driver mumbled something and slammed his door.

"You sure?"

"Yes, I'm good. Let me know when you make it to Michigan."

"I will, love you." She patted my strawberry blond hair.

"Love you too, Mama. Have a good flight." I stood there on the sidewalk waving until he turned off the street. Putting my hand on my hip I shook my head looking at the ground. What in the world is going on? That was so confusing, it sure looked like Mr. Wolf. Why is he trying to mess with me? Enough of this! I needed to call Charlie.

As soon I stepped into the foyer, the kitchen phone rang loudly. Darting over I snatched up the receiver, "Hello?"

"Hi, are you looking for an adventure? Guess who's back in town?" Charlie asked.

"My life is an adventure. I think you should know that by now! Wait, are you here?"

"No, not me, but I'm coming for you later today," Charlie joked.

"I look forward to it," I said in a playful tone.

"Father Beau is back," he told me.

"Finally! Oh, and I must tell you what happened sending Mama off to the airport when you get here. Things are getting wild."

Charlie arrived at the house later that day when I was on the phone with Mama, "I'm glad you made it safe to Michigan, Mama. Hold on, I need to get to the front door," I said, putting the phone on the kitchen counter.

"Hi Charlie," I whispered sweetly, peeking around the door, opening it for him to enter, "I'm on the phone with Mama." I darted off leaving him to close the door and make himself at home. Picking up the phone I said, "I'm back Mama." He came into the kitchen pouring himself a cup of coffee and sitting at the bistro table set.

"Who's there, Dixie?" Mama asked.

"No, it's Charlie. I'm visiting Dixie again later."

"Tell him hello for me."

"Mama says hello," I said cupping the speaker and looking at him sipping his coffee waiting patiently.

"Hello Mama Kaye," he spoke over the rim of the coffee mug as if she were in the room with us.

"He said hi. Okay, I'll let you go. Tell everyone I love them."

"Still wish you were here," she said.

"I know. Next time," I said with a slight eye roll. "Bye Mama."

"Bye sweetie."

I put the receiver back on the cradle, "Are you ready to go see Father Beau?" I asked Charlie.

"Am I ready? I think I should be asking you. Are you ready?"

"You know what I mean," I gave his shoulder a little shove, "Are you ready to roll out? Jeeze."

"You're a little feisty this morning, aren't you?"

"Maybe," I said putting my coffee cup and plate in the sink, "come on let's go." I took the mug from him and rinsed it and put it with mine in the sink.

"I wasn't done with that," he protested.

"You're now," I laughed and pushed him from the bistro seat to his feet.

"I feel like you want to get going?" He stood like a brick wall as I pushed him to try to get him to move.

"Okay then, I'm going without you!" I stomped off and left him in the kitchen. He didn't follow so I returned and peeked my head around the doorframe, "Seriously, I want to go."

He chuckled and followed me. "Okay, the jeep's parked out front on the sidewalk, we probably should leave before I get a ticket."

CHAPTER EIGHTEEN

Back to Father Beau

I clicked my seat belt and adjusted it making it more comfortable. Since it was still chilly, Charlie had the top up and door on the Jeep. The hum of the wheels on the road helped me drift away to remember some sweet memories.

As we approached the church, Charlie slowed, and the hum of the tires changed. The crunch of the oyster shells brought the jeep to a stop. Parking the Jeep, he reached over he placed his right hand on my left forearm, "Are you ready? You know what questions you are going to ask Father Beau?"

"I have a slight outline in my head."

"Sounds like a typical plan." He patted my arm and laughed lightly, "Come on, let's go see him."

As usual the front doors were unlocked. The brilliant sunlight beamed through the stained-glass windows casting beautiful patterns of color throughout the church. We made our way to the office. I tapped twice on the door, twisted the doorknob, and called into the room, "Father Beau?"

"Arielle! Please come in." The calming voice of Father Beau called to me, "Ms. Marie said you'd be back to visit with me."

As Charlie and I entered, my shoulders relaxed upon seeing Father Beau, "I'm so glad to see you."

"It's always a pleasure. Hi Charlie." Father Beau extended his hand giving Charlie a firm pump, "Please take a seat." With his hand open and palm up he gestured to the table and chairs.

I chose my seat and Charlie sat next to me. I watched Father walk around to one of the two empty seats and sit. He folded his hands and placed them on the table. Smiling gently at me, "Ms. Marie isn't in the office today. She needed a few days off after working very hard while I was out."

"I'll have to come back and see her another time," I told Father Beau as I crossed my legs at the ankle trying to be as poised as I could.

"She does enjoy sharing her scones and tea with you. So, tell me what has been going on with you," he said with arms and hands open with emphasis as if he were about to hug me, but he kept boundaries and his hands returned to their folded position on the table.

I started from the beginning with the funeral for Aunt Nina. "I was supposed to meet Father Verum behind St. Louis Cathedral in the garden. He wasn't there when I arrived, and I got distracted by something rustling in the bushes." I recalled.

Father Beau just nodded, keeping his hands folded on the table. His brow slightly furrowed he would blink rapidly, then relax trying to take in everything.

"I was struck from behind and when I woke up Papa's book and Aunt Nina's books were gone. I missed the burial of Aunt Nina," I said, wiping a tear from my cheek that escaped. "I'm sorry; I'm just upset."

Father Beau unfolded his hands and reached across the table and grabbed my right hand giving it a quick squeeze. "I can't imagine what you are feeling. Go on when you are ready." He encouraged me then released my hand.

Taking a shaky breath, I composed myself and continued, "Well, fast forward. I found out that Father Verum stole my books! And then gave them away to this awful person whom I call Mr. Wolf."

"Wait, are you telling me Father Verum took your books?" Father Beau asked, drawing back in his chair.

"Yes, he admitted it to me! I don't understand why Father Verum and Mr. Wolf are stealing books together. It seemed like they have been working together for quite some time."

Father Beau composed himself and began, "Arielle, I'm not saying you are mistaken, I'm just trying to understand everything. Are you sure?"

My eyes filled with tears, and I fought to keep them from spilling down my cheeks. Not able to speak, I just took a few deep breaths. Great, Father Beau doesn't believe me either, now what am I going to do? I trusted Father Beau, but then again, I had trusted Father

Verum too and look where that got me? I glanced at Charlie to see if he was thinking the same thing I was.

"Hey. It's okay. We're going to figure this out," Charlie said, putting his hand on my shoulder.

"Arielle, I'm not trying to upset you, I just need to know all the details to figure this out with you. Let's take it slow." Father continued to ask me questions dissecting the whole encounter. He wanted to know when I first figured out who Mr. Wolf was, how I found the shop and why he wasn't at the shop anymore. Did I go back to the shop again? Have I seen Father Verum again?

I looked at Charlie for assurance and he nodded for me to trust him and gave me a soft smile. Taking my time to revisit the events, I looked for things I may have missed and answered Father Beau's questions. Our conversation continued for about two hours. Father started to recap our conversation and I interrupted him, "Do you have some water?"

"Absolutely, I was so engrossed in where our conversation was going, excuse me." He rose and returned with a pitcher and three tall clear glasses on one of Ms. Marie's ornate trays. We sat and drank in silence.

"Okay let's get this figured out," he said, clapping his hands together once. Excitedly, he spun from his chair going to one of his many bookshelves. There were rows and rows of leather-bound books. The wealth of information was endless. Father Beau pulled two books and set them on the table. Then returned to the bookshelves and scanned the books with his index finger. He retrieved one more book from the shelves and brought it over to us.

I wanted to crack open the book and start flipping through it to find something, so I sat on my hand to keep myself under control. Father picked up a deep maroon book first and gently thumbed through the pages. He left it open and placed it on the table. Then picking up one of the two black bound books he did the same thing. After placing the second book open on the table he continued to the last book.

I wobbled on my hands trying to get some blood flow back to them. "Can I help you find anything?" I asked after waiting, unable to hold back my anxiousness.

160

"I think I found a few things," he answered basically saying no, just wait.

Charlie sipped his water and leaned back in the chair. I mouthed the words to him "I'm sorry." He shrugged and smiled to say, "Don't worry."

"Okay, let's look at this first," Father said. He stood and pulled a chair next to me and put the book on the table for us to both see better.

Grabbing the seat of the chair I hopped forward to get closer to the book. "What are we looking at or for?"

"I think there might be a few explanations. You said Father Verum told you he took your books to keep you safe?"

"Yes, but why give them to Mr. Wolf when he knew he was going to just come after me?"

"Okay, Mr. Wolf is shown here." Father pointed to a hand drawing of a wolf wearing the exact same hat.

"Holy shit!" I said, then quickly clamping my mouth wide eyed looking at Father Beau.

"We will do confession after this," he said sternly.

"I'm sorry I'll do better, please continue."

"So, Mr. Wolf is an evil spirit that has been around for many generations. He is a dimensional being that moves freely. He is dangerous and he can be fatal. His name is actually Fenris. He was bound by a rope, and once he broke free, he has been traveling in and out of our world for quite some time now. I didn't know he was here again."

"I don't like the sound of this. But why would Father Verum give him my books?"

"I think he knew that Mr. Wolf, as you call him, was coming for the books. He is a bit of a collector, you might say. He has even visited here and taken from my collection. Maybe he was really trying to keep you safe, by taking them first and removing you from the unknown harm?" Father Beau suggested.

"Why would there be pages missing from Papa's book when I got it back?" I asked.

"Your Papa was a very smart man. There have been rumors that he was working on a spell to unlock any book. Do you remember reading anything like that in his book?"

"No, but I have learned that not everything is revealed at the same time. Maybe I wasn't supposed to see it yet?"

"That's possible," Father Beau agreed.

"Do you think that Father Verum or Mr. Wolf has the pages?"

"Perhaps Mr. Wolf has the pages and needs you to read them to open Aunt Nina's book?"

"Maybe, but I was able to get the item to open Aunt Nina's book, but we are the only ones that know," I said drawing a circle with my finger between Charlie, Father, and myself.

"That's exciting and maybe something you should keep quiet about."

"What makes me mad is Father Verum could have warned me, I could have defeated Mr. Wolf." I said with arms crossed and my brow furrowed pouting like a child.

"Arielle, right now you do not display the signs of a mature fighter," Father Beau pointed out honestly.

My eyes fluttered realizing I was acting like a brat, "Maybe you are right." Changing the subject away from myself I asked, "What else did you find?"

He placed the book down on the other side of the table and reached for one of the black leather books. "This one's interesting," he said, putting the book on the table in front of us like he did with the maroon one. "You talked about Ms. LuLu at the River Road Plantation?"

Charlie sat up straight and put his empty glass on the table next to mine. "What about her?" This was the first time Charlie had engaged in our conversation.

"How familiar are you with Ms. LuLu?" Father asked Charlie.

162

"Very, I have known her my entire life. Why?"

"You know she is also an interdimensional being?" Father shared with Charlie leaning over to see his face to read his reaction.

Charlie stared at the empty glass not speaking.

"Charlie? Have you noticed she really has not aged over the time you have known her?"

Charlie blinked slowly and turned to face me, "I think I need a minute." He looked at Father Beau, "You can continue, but I'm not answering any questions."

I patted Charlie's arm and gave it a squeeze acknowledging he was now feeling what I usually am going through.

"Well Ms. LuLu is a very special person and great to have on your side. She has the ability to predict and share the future or anything else you might need to see to put you on your correct path in life." Father glanced up to look at Charlie who was deep in thought. "She can also move between time and space like Fenris, I mean uh, Mr. Wolf. If she indeed is going to help you, she might be able to help you find him. However, her powers are not helpful in a battle."

"She said she wanted to help me, and she also said she saw what happened to me with Jacob, my angel. Ms. LuLu couldn't see beyond the oak trees when Mr. Wolf tried to bring me into another world."

"That brings me to the last book." Father Beau closed the current book, placed it to the side, and picked up the last thick book. "Look at this section." He pointed to a drawing.

Charlie interrupted us, "Can I look at the one about Ms. LuLu?"

"Of course." Father pointed to the book, "I think she is around page 280?" He guessed and turned his attention back to me "There's a cloud showing a wall between two people. Can you memorize this?" There was a hand scripted sentence under the image.

"What does it say?"

Father Beau picked up the book, pulling it closer to him he placed the heavy book on his lap, "This is a good one for you to remember."

He adjusted his thin reading glasses on the tip of his nose tilting his head back a little to line up his eyes with the lines to read out loud,

"Eyes of mine,

I can see just fine.

Blind away the view of you,

giving them no clue."

"What does it do?" I asked before trying to memorize it.

"It is an old spell that will blind others from seeing what is going on from one direction. Mr. Wolf most probably used this knowing Ms. LuLu was there and watching."

"What a snake!" I said glaring at the book.

Charlie joked, laughing at himself, "No, he's a wolf."

"Really? You joining the conversation again?" I asked, picking back at him.

"Yes, I'm okay, I just need to process. Sorry, please continue. I won't interrupt again," he smiled.

Father Beau handed me the book to put in my lap. I took the book and almost dropped it in my lap from the weight. I used my index finger to read along in my head. Closing my eyes, I repeated to myself without looking. After a few minutes I asked Father Beau, "So, how do I know it is working? I say the words, but maybe I speak one word wrong and I think they can't see me, but they can?"

Father put his hand out to take the book back from me. I grab it tight, lifting it to him. He continued to read from the spell, flipping the page he read to the bottom of the page then paused. "Here is something interesting. The spell creates a color boundary."

He flipped back to the image tapping his finger on the page, "You see the wall drawn here? That will be a color. The book doesn't say what color. Imagine a colored wall that prevents anything on the

164

other side of the wall from being seen." He drew an imaginary semi-circle around the wall, "However, if you walk around the wall, you can see everything," Father Beau explained.

"Okay, that makes sense. Thank you for trying to piece this together. Where do you think Father Verum is?" I directed my question to Father Beau, but watching Charlie completely engrossed in the book with Ms. LuLu in it again.

Father Beau followed my view and asked Charlie a question instead of answering me, "Charlie, are you learning anything new about Ms. LuLu?"

"Maybe not new per se, but things make more sense about her. I knew she was an amazing person, but I didn't know how amazing."

"Has she ever said you might have something special about you?" Father Beau prodded.

"Maybe," Charlie said without giving up any more information and keeping his eyes on the book.

"I guess we can touch on that subject another day?" Father Beau asked with a hopeful tone in his voice.

"Maybe," he said again, trying not to be disrespectful, but honest.

"Arielle, what'd you ask me before?" Changing the focus back on me. "Oh, wait I remember, how could I forget? Where could Father Verum be?"

"Yes, I was thinking you might have an idea?"

"I doubt he is hiding; he does have a church he tends to. Maybe if you spend some time with Ms. LuLu, she can give you some insight?"

"That is a great idea. I hope these dark days can be behind me soon."

"Arielle, they can be, keep yourself centered in Christ. Be like His light to defeat the darkness. You possess great power and abilities but need more direction."

165

"Be still and let your light shine," I repeated what Aunt Nina told me.

"Exactly."

"Charlie, how're you doing over there?" I asked.

"I'm up to my eyeballs in information. I'm good."

"You ready to go back to River Road Plantation?"

Father interjected, "Charlie you are free to come back anytime and use the library, and we can chat too."

"Thank you, Father, I'll keep that in mind." Not wanting to commit to anything, "Yes I'm ready to go when you are."

We thanked Father for the long session of learning and headed out. "Also, if I'm not here you can always rely on Father Guidry, he might be younger, but don't let that fool you. His knowledge is great about these matters. Next time, you should meet him."

"I'm willing to add any help to my circle. I'm just a little cautious after all this stuff with Father Verum."

"As you should be," Father Beau agreed.

The sun was starting to drop in the sky. A cool breeze swirled around us, raising my hair straight in the sky. We found warmth in the jeep. Charlie cranked the engine and with one palm on the steering wheel he drove us out onto the main road.

"Where are we going now?" I asked.

"Dinner." Is all he offered up.

I smiled and let him take control.

CHAPTER NINETEEN

Safe in His Arms

We sat in silence taking in all the things we just learned from Father Beau. Charlie knew I didn't like to be out at night alone, so I was glad he was with me. Too many creepy things get amplified during the night. He turned down the street next to St. Louis Cemetery Number 2. My cheek pressed against the jeep window looking up at the tall white cement wall that forms the boundary of the cemetery. The cement creatures were perched along the top. Their heads moved watching us drive by. I sat back quickly in the seat keeping my eyes forward.

Charlie pressed the radio button changing the station to the current hit B 97.1 with the volume on low. I placed my hand over my stomach to try to reassure it would eat again. We pulled into a parallel parking spot on the street. I took my time unclipping my seat belt while he pressed coins in the meter for our spot. He tapped on the window before he opened my door to ask. "You coming? I know you are hungry."

I gave him a weak smile and a single nod. Stepping onto the curb he wrapped his arm around my waist. "What's going on with you? I'm here."

"I know, just feeling a little creeped out," I admitted, without telling him about the cast of creatures at the nearby cemetery. I was waiting for them to pop up next to us.

"We're not going far, there is a great place I want to take you to."

I leaned into his chest and matched his steps so we could walk close together.

He stopped in front of a green and yellow wrought iron designed sign and released me from his grasp to point up at the sign, which read 'Arnaud's'. "You are going to love this place." The deep red pillars housed gas light lamps that flickered in the cold night.

"Cool. I haven't been here yet."

"Good, let's unwind and have a great meal." He held the door open and gestured for me to enter. I froze from moving forward into the restaurant when a blast of cold air hit me from behind and split my hair creating a part along the back of my head.

Quickly Charlie put his hand on the small of my back and pushed me forward into the restaurant. I spun around and looked while Charlie blocked the continuing blast and swung the wooden door shut. I peeked over Charlie's broad shoulder through the yellow glass and saw Mr. Wolf. He evaporated into a grey mist.

"Charlie, he's right outside," I whispered in his ear while still looking outside. My voice cracked trying to say his name.

"Arielle, I've got you. I'm not going to let anyone or anything hurt you." He whispered back.

"He's…" I whimpered.

"Good, let's try not letting him rule our lives."

"This has consumed my life," I continued to whisper in his ear.

Charlie wrapped his arms around me. "We're safe here; this is a dwelling for good only."

I nodded, remembering that in the past there were locations that both angels and demons would be and some places they couldn't overlap.

"Uh um," a man cleared his throat to get our attention.

We peeled apart greeting a host dressed in a tuxedo. Realizing this is a very fancy place, I looked down at my clothes and pressed them to release any possible wrinkles.

"You looking to dine here tonight?" the host asked with a sneer.

"Yes, a table for two please." Charlie requested holding up his index and middle finger wrapping his other arm around my waist.

"We do not permit seating unless you are properly dressed," the host said, turning his face away in slight disgust of our attire.

"Yes, I totally understand…" Charlie began to say.

"Charlie, come on, let's go somewhere else," I said quietly.

"No, it's alright," he said, turning his face toward mine.

"I beg to differ. It's not alright," the host said with sharpness. Waving his hand up and down emphasizing Charlies' wardrobe, "You aren't allowed to eat here unless you have a jacket and tie."

"Thank you for your insight, sir. Can I please speak to Chef Dino?" Charlie requested.

"Chef Dino?"

"Yes, Chef Dino."

"Whom may I say is asking?" the host asked, squirming a little.

"Just say Charlie-o."

"Very well." The host spun on his heels and trotted off.

I smiled weakly at Charlie. He winked at me and gave me a squeeze with this arm wrapped around me.

A jolly guy around our age came bouncing out. Charlie let go of me as the guy wrapped his arms around Charlie and sang, "Char-lie-ooo! How are you, man?"

"Fantastic, Dino, how are you?"

Dino backed away and glanced at me giving Charlie a little elbow in his side, "You must be doing well, who do you have here?"

Charlie almost blushed, "This is Arielle."

Dino grasped my hand, bending forward and planted a kiss on my hand, "My lady."

I squeaked, "Hi." drawing my hand up to my neck.

"You here to dine tonight?" Dino asked.

"We did pop in and are hungry, but…" Charlie looked down at this plain T-shirt and blue jeans.

Dino tapped his lips, "I see. We do have a dress code, ya know?" he said in his thick Italian accent.

"Quite a predicament we are in, aren't we?" Charlie asked, glancing at me.

Dino clapped his hands together a few times, "I'll be right back."

Charlie gave the host a nod and a huge smile as Dino darted off.

The host pressed his lips creating a fine line and went back behind his podium.

"Here, try this on." Dino waved a jacket at Charlie, "This should fit you just fine. Here is a tie too! Much better!"

Charlie adjusted the tie and turned for my approval. I beamed at how handsome he looked.

"Very good!" Dino said, fluttering his hands toward the host's station, "Come, come this way. Please seat them at once."

The host gave a slight eye roll that Dino didn't see, "Of course, right this way," he said dryly.

Charlie held his hand out for me to follow. We walked through a bar area. The floor was covered with tiny tiles leading us into one of the dining areas. The walls were decorated with a soft mint green and cream wallpaper.

The round tables each had a crisp white tablecloth adorned with white peaks of napkins. Gorgeous multicolored roses towered atop the center of the tables. Charlie took my hand as I looked at the ceilings which housed clear boxes filled with candles.

Charlie gazed into my eyes. I looked away sheepishly as my cheeks flushed. I thought about us and our lives. I really had fallen in love with Charlie. I wanted to be with him all the time, but he lived in the swamp and I was in the city. Our worlds didn't mesh right now. I couldn't ask him to leave his home when I'd finally found my path. The next step in our relationship could wait since we both were not ready to make changes to our lives. I needed to be with the people of New Orleans. He needed to be teaching kids about alligators. Couldn't his cousin Nick take care of this? I didn't want to wait any longer and be without him. We had to find a middle ground; it just wasn't time for our love to blossom any further. The internal fight continued as we shared our evening together, we didn't speak of our underlying love for each other because we couldn't be together yet. The timing was off. Absence

170

makes the heart grow fonder they say, but we couldn't make our bond stronger if we were not together.

I sighed and gazed at him feeling the sweet, romantic atmosphere. "Once again Charlie, you have surprised me."

He chuckled, "We have known each other for a long time, but I'm ready to let you into my life completely."

"I like that," I said softly.

The waiter interrupted my gaze and filled our water glasses. "Good evening, my name is Rey. Could I interest you in an appetizer tonight? And are we celebrating anything this evening?"

"Everything looks amazing. What do you suggest?" I asked our waiter.

"The Shrimp Arnaud is a classic and one of my personal favorites," he suggested.

I glanced at Charlie, "What do you think?"

"Go for it," he encouraged me.

"Okay, that sounds like a winner to me."

I sought Charlie's opinion about my entree selection as the waiter breezed away into the kitchen, "I am looking at the crab cakes, what about you?"

"I was thinking about the Gulf Fish Duarte."

"Oh, that looks heavenly with a little spice."

"Just like I like my women," he smirked.

I gave him a sharp smack on his arm. "You know you like me just the way I am."

"I do, I do!" he said, holding both palms up to make me stop.

Charlie continued the conversation after our appetizer, "Arielle, I have lost most of my family and you mean the world to me, you know that, right?"

I blinked slowly, enjoying his kind words. "Yes."

"I know this isn't the right place or time, but I just feel moved to ask you..."

I could feel my heart start to race in anticipation of his next sentence.

Charlie leaned back with his hands in his lap. The waiter placed our plates in front of each of us. "Bon Appetit! Anything else you require?"

"Looks great to me," I managed to squeak out.

Charlie gave him a thumbs up. He picked up his fork and knife and cut a small piece of the filet. He paused right before he put the food in his mouth and glanced at me. I sat very still waiting and watching him. I told myself to be still. I concentrated on my breathing mostly to remind myself to continue breathing while I waited for Charlie to finish his sentence. Charlie was amused and took his bite with a grin. I waited with my hand placed properly in my lap on the cloth napkin.

When Charlie went to cut another bite, I filled the silence by clearing my throat and continued to blink slowly at him. He gently put his utensils down and placed his palms on the top of the table gazing at me. The waiter breezed over to ask, "Are we good over here? Dino will be out shortly to talk to you."

Trying to be patient I said, "Everything is lovely. Thank you." And I picked up my fork to begin my meal and concentrated solely on my food. "Oh wow, this is so good!" I said to Charlie, glancing at him.

He grinned, "Yes I agree, Dino really has some amazing food here."

"I guess you're done with your subject from earlier?" I probed.

Dino bustled over to our table clasping his hands together he proclaimed, "Friends!"

"Chef Dino, thank you so much for an amazing meal," Charlie smiled back at him.

"It really is one of the best meals I have ever had, but don't tell my mama," I joked.

Dino winked and pointed at me, "Ah, yes! No one is better than Mama! I will leave you two kiddos but wanted to stop by and say how nice it is to see you, Charlie and to meet you, Arielle."

Alone again, I took another bite of my crab cakes and gave Charlie a side glance.

He smiled at me, "I love you, Arielle."

"I figured you did after all the craziness I put you through," I joked, then turning serious I continued, "I love you too, Charlie."

He reached out an open hand across the table. I put my fork down and reached to place my hand in his. "I'm not really a fancy kind of guy, but I want you to have all the best in life, Arielle."

I nodded. *Don't forget to breathe,* I told myself.

"I am not really prepared for this either, but I realized that I want to spend the rest of my life with you," Charlie admitted, squeezing my hand. "I'm not sure how we will do this, but I can't see myself with anyone else."

I started to blush and beamed, "I love you, Charlie." I looked down at our clasped hands trying to contain my excitement.

"I don't have the ring with me, but I know exactly what I am going to give you," Charlie said, rubbing his thumb over my ring finger then releasing my hand. "I didn't know I was going to ask you tonight, but I don't know why I'm waiting." He paused, getting down on one knee and asked, "So, Arielle Mathis, will you marry me?"

Leaning over the table our lips met for a long time, "Yes," I whispered. "If you think you can handle all of the things that come with me!" I joked.

"You have no idea. I can't wait for this journey with you," he kissed me gently and sat back in his chair.

Dino came out with all the staff cheering, whistling, and hollering, "Congratulations!" Patting Charlie on the shoulder and sweet smiles toward me. Even the host came over and gave a stiff bow with a short, "Congratulations to you both."

All the stress of life melted away in that moment. I felt safe with Charlie. Even if he didn't know how to protect me from demons, he would do anything in his power to keep me safe. I leaned across the table for another kiss, "I love you, Charlie."

"I love you too, Arielle and I'm ready for this chapter to unfold. I'm here to help you. I'm excited to be a real part of your journey. God has some amazing things in store for you."

"No." I corrected him, "God has some amazing things in store for us!"

"Okay, I'll agree with that." He lifted his water glass to clink mine. "Are you going to go all out planning this wedding?"

"Define all out."

"I don't care what the wedding is like, but I'd like to have it at the plantation," he suggested.

"It would be beautiful, wouldn't it?"

"I think we'd be able to have more of our family there than the living, if you understand what I am saying," Charlie explained.

"I do understand, and I think that would be beautiful as long as the rest stay out," I warned.

"I'll make sure you are safe," he promised.

"Okay, I guess I am planning a wedding and getting Aunt Nina's book back. I can do this," I said.

"Will you let me ask your Mama before you tell her? I know I wasn't able to ask your Papa, but I think she would appreciate it."

"Yes, that would make her happy," I agreed, "But can I tell Dixie?"

"If you think she will keep it quiet," he said.

"Well, I think she will since I have some dirt on her," I winked at him.

"Oh, jeez what have y'all been up too?" he asked with a worried look.

"Not me! It's all her. Well, her and Ernie if you get my drift."

"Don't tell me. I don't want to be involved. You know I am a terrible liar. If anyone asked me anything, I'd spill the beans," Charlie admitted.

I put my index finger over my pursed lips as if to say Shhhh.

CHAPTER TWENTY

Crystal

A soft cool breeze fluttered around my face; the white puffy clouds streamed by in the periwinkle blue sky. Holding my left-hand fingers stretched out I smiled slightly, remembering Charlie putting the ring on my finger when we got back to the plantation last night. It was his grandmother's ring. The oval opal was surrounded by ten smaller opals creating a cluster of iridescent colors. Each of the ten smaller opals displayed a different shade of color. My eyes rested on the teal blue one, which is my favorite.

A shadow flickered from above distracting my focus on the ring. I raised my open hand to cover the glare of the sun watching as a great blue heron gliding through the sky with his five-foot wingspan. He gracefully drifted over the cypress trees heading to the bayou located on the back of the plantation property. I found a cement bench to rest on, which was a little chilly through my denim jeans. I sat trying to be still and let my light shine.

Distracted by the sounds around me, I watched the winds rustle the brown leaves across the ground as they tumbled over the fading green grass. It was unseasonably warm for this time of year. I decided to take a walk along the winding garden path.

I spotted the groundskeeper off in the distance burning a pile of leaves. The smokey smell of burning leaves drifted over to my nose. It reminded me of my childhood when we would sit around the fireplace in our home on Royal Street.

Papa would start a fire and give us a metal stick with a wooden handle. Gathered around the crackling flames Mama would pop a white puffy marshmallow on the end for us to roast. My brother, Mark, would let his catch fire before pulling it out and blowing on it to extinguish it.

I preferred a light brown toasting rather than a scorched black, burnt marshmallow. Taking my index finger and thumb I would give the puff a gentle squeeze to pull on the stick. The gooey white melted center pulled away, dripping in a thin string. I popped it in my mouth and squeezed the soft marshmallow between my teeth feeling it push through the cracks to my cheeks. My tongue pushed out to catch the sticky on my lips. A big smile formed from the sweetness.

Just then, peeping sounds from a small bird turned my attention to somewhere in the trees along the path. I kept my head still and used my eyes to scan the trees that surrounded me. Looking for any movement to spot the bird calling for his mate. The large green palm fronds danced in the breeze, their thin tips curled down to the earth showing the weathering of the seasons. The ends waved to me as if to say, your birdie is not here, keep looking. Closing my eyes, I listened for his call again. My nose filled with the earthy smells around me. I could tell a storm was not too far away from the musky wet dirt smell. I gave a slight cough to clear the smell.

Keeping my eyes closed I heard peep, peep, peep to my left. I snapped my head a quarter of a turn darting my eyes to spot him. The branches swayed gently in the breeze, but I still couldn't find him. I closed my eyes again and quietly breathed deeply. This time I could catch a hint of the pine trees nearby.

The sounds of peep, peep, peep, brought me back to my search for the unidentified bird. Where is that little guy? I looked again for any motion, keeping still, but scanning with my eyes. A red flash bolted among the branches. I turned my shoulders to face directly at the tree with few green leaves still on it. There you are! A small red cardinal appeared; he hopped over to a leafless branch to show his full red body. He cocked his head left and right watching me.

"Hi little guy," I spoke softly to him.

He peeped once back at me. Keeping my eyes fixed on him I took a step forward and the twigs below my boots snapped them into little bits over the dead grass. The cardinal flapped his wings and flew up to a section of branches higher in the tree. I stopped and folded my hands near my belly and stood waiting to see where he would go next. He turned back to face me with a peep, peep.

"I'm coming closer," I told him.

I looked down and examined the millions of tiny branches that I was about to pulverize. The constant loud crunch continued until I stopped at the base of the tree. I looked up to find my new friend, but I couldn't see him anymore. I rested my hand on the grey bark and listened.

Peep, peep, peep, he told me he was still there. I stepped back over the broken twigs looking up again. The trees beyond this one danced in the wind, but this one remained still. The cardinal hopped along a branch coming into view. I walked around the base of the tree to see him better. Once he saw I was following him, he fluttered to the next large tree.

I made eye contact with him and looked back down to watch my step as I followed him to the next tree. This was another small tree with tiny branches. It was easy for me to see him since most of the leaves had fallen. I met him at the next tree. Then he peeped at me three more times and flew quite a distance this time but remained where I could see him.

I glanced back at my trail knowing I was going off the path, but I was intrigued to see where the bird was leading me. The sun was still showing so I knew it was only about mid-day. Catching up to him again he peeped and flew very far, this time I couldn't find him, and the trees were starting to become denser.

"I don't see you anymore," I wandered a bit, still seeing nothing.

I closed my eyes and listened. The cold breeze moved through the trees as more brown leaves fell swirling to the ground. I couldn't smell the rain coming anymore, but the pine was very strong. I ran my fingers through my hair, fluffing it up and scratching my head a bit. My index finger on my left hand found a sticky patch. Sap attack! From a pine tree, I pulled the hair away for my now sticky fingers. Patting the sap on my jeans I tried to get the sticky sap to fade away some.

Peep. Leaving the rest of the sap on my fingers I searched for the cardinal, there he was! I climbed over a fallen tree and slipped down onto the other side. Once my feet were planted on the ground I looked back wondering if I should turn back. The cardinal came to me and perched on the fallen tree close enough so that I could reach out and touch him. He hopped up and down to get me to look at him.

"Where're we going?" I asked him.

He flew off continuing our journey. I used my palm to move the draping vines and continued to crunch my way over the fallen twigs. The cardinal landed on the top of a gate. The hinges on the left side were

178

broken off the top part and one open rusted door rested on the earth. It had been there awhile embedded in the earth. The other door of the gate was inviting us to come on in. The cardinal rested upon the top of the gate at the point of a fleur de lis.

He peeped at me a few more times. I came closer, examining the area and figuring out where the gate took us. There was an arch that came into view, it was about twelve feet tall and inside the metal arch were the words St. Michael's Cemetery.

I stood frozen. I didn't know where I was and not sure what I might encounter inside this old, abandoned cemetery. *What have I gotten myself into?* I thought.

I looked squarely at the cardinal, "Are you friend or foe?" I asked him point blankly. Realizing this should have been established long ago.

The cardinal breezed over and landed on my shoulder. My vision changed as the rust from the cemetery gates floated away. The hinge opened and the screws that were missing appeared and twisted into place putting the gate back where it needed to be. The grass curled from the brown dead grass to a lush vibrant green. The one missing iron letter from the arch, a "C", floated down, completing the word Cemetery. I stood still watching the old cemetery come back to life.

The dead vines that wound up the entrance gate and around the fences pulled away and faded into the new green grass. The broken part of the picket fence mended itself and the mossy grey green fence turned a brilliant white color like it was when it was fresh and new. Beyond the perimeter I looked inside, the main rectangular grave stood tall in the middle topped by an angel. The weather had worn down the top of her wings and the nose. Her wings were covered with green moss.

The statue came to life and spread her wings, flapping away the moss. She tossed her head removing the decades of pollen and debris that rested on her. She tapped her heels one by one and the moss fell off. Taking her hands, she spread out her gown removing the mildewed spots that have grown over the years. She twisted around to check her wings making sure she was presentable.

179

She didn't know the cardinal and I were watching her as she continued to groom herself, returning to her original splendor. Her fingertips brushed over her eyes giving her better sight. The angel ran her hand over her face bringing her delicate nose back to a soft point. The cardinal let out a loud peep. She turned slowly to look at us. I froze, not sure if she could see me or if I only could see her.

She opened her wings and flapped them, removing the last of the gunk that had settled on her over the years. She flew up showing her bare feet and pointed them down at the grave and landed. She gazed at us and used her hand to gesture. I took a step closer as the bird flew from my shoulder. The cemetery flickered and showed a glimpse of the disaster it had become for a split second then returned to its splendor.

The cardinal landed on a grave just inside the gate and turned back to me. The sun was getting a little lower in the sky as the clouds continued to scroll past creating shadows on the cemetery. I walked to the now perfect gate and paused in the entrance. I gazed around before entering. The cardinal perched upon a single white cross, the bright white of the cross with the beautiful green grass around it really made his red color pop.

This cemetery had about a dozen crosses marking the in-ground graves. A variety of tombs all were above ground, as they should be in Southeast Louisiana.

The angel extended her hand out and the bird landed on her palm. I decided to continue to follow the bird and greet the angel. She turned her gaze to me. I gingerly walked avoiding stepping the few in ground graves because I didn't want to disturb anyone that might be resting. I approached the center of the cemetery and looked up at the angel. She was sitting on the edge of the tall tomb with her delicate white feet dangling down at me. She smiled and waved. Now that I was closer, I could see she was larger than I realized.

"Hello," I said almost in a whisper.

Her soft buttery voice responded, "Hello, Arielle."

I was surprised she knew my name, but I shouldn't have been. Things were always unpredictable in my life. "What do I call you?" I asked.

"My name is Crystal," she said, folding her wings to cascade around the front of her body.

"How old are you? I mean how old is this cemetery?"

She placed her hand on either side of her hips and pushed off. Her wings opened wide as she floated down to the ground. She stood about nine feet tall. Folding her wings behind her she cupped her hands together. "I was placed here the early part of the nineteenth century in your time, but I am timeless."

"Why were you placed here?"

"I'm one of God's messengers. I know no bounds, but for today's purpose I live here waiting for you to come to me. Once my purpose is fulfilled, I'll be able to leave this statue and move onto my next mission."

"So, you have been here for all this time waiting for me?"

"Yes, I have been waiting for you, but don't worry, my idea of time and space isn't the same as yours."

"I have a feeling tonight's going to feel like a very long night for me," I told her.

"Yes, I'm sure it'll be for you." She knelt on the grass and ran her fingers over the blades. Watching them bend and bounce back up.

"You're not a statue, but an angel, so why do you look like an angel?" I asked.

"For humans this is my natural form, a statue, but I have a little color for those who can really see me." She laughed looking at her arms, "This color is quite drab."

"Can I see you in your real form?" I asked.

"I don't know if that is a good idea." She warned, "I could be a little, um, intimidating."

"I'm sure I have seen worse. Okay, then why don't you explain why you are waiting for me instead?"

"Of course, I was sent by God to wait here for you to tell you this." She paused for effect, "Be still and let your light shine." She clapped her cement hands together causing the sound of bricks being smashed together.

My brow furrowed as I rolled my eyes and looked right, not making eye contact with her anymore. "You're kidding, right?"

Turning her back to me and bouncing from the ground leaving the grass flattened from her weight. She landed on top of the grave and moved so I couldn't see her anymore. I backed away realizing I was not being very receptive.

I called to her, "Crystal, I'm sorry. I was expecting something a little more profound since you have been waiting so long."

Still out of view her voice responded, "It's exactly what you need to hear and do. No matter what you think."

I folded my arms and turned away from her. Now what. I was still and nothing was happening. What does God want from me? He could be a little more direct than continuing with this same vague message. Be still and let your light shine. What does that even mean?

I turned back to look. I could only see her feet along the edge of the grave top. With the sweetest voice I could make I asked, "What does it mean? I'm sitting here waiting and nothing is happening."

Her feet moved away from the edge. I could hear her moving around up there, but still couldn't see her. Her head peeked over the edge. I could see her flower crown was a little off to the left. Her cheeks appeared to be puffy. Could this statue, this angel, have her feelings hurt? She didn't answer me and disappeared again.

"I'm sorry. That was rude of me. You're just trying to deliver a message to me."

Her soft voice said, "Exactly what you have been doing for years, has anyone treated you the way you treated me?" she asked pointedly.

"No, not really, but I haven't been giving messages lately either."

"You really think that's the point I'm trying to make?"

182

"No." I said humbly, "I'm really sorry. Can you come back down here? I'll play nice, I promise."

She was airborne before I could finish my sentence. Her large wings pumped in the sky as she circled the small cemetery not leaving the invisible walls that held her inside. She blew off some steam and touched down near me facing away. She was not as close as the first time she came down from her grave top. I walked to her and gently touched her cement wing that was now folded behind her. I was surprised that her wing felt like soft feathers but looked like a dense stone statue. She pulled her wing away from me and turned to show the hurt in her face.

I dropped my hand to my side, "Will you forgive me, Crystal?" I pleaded quietly, "I was insensitive, and I'm truly sorry."

"Do you know how important your role is in this world?" She asked. "You have messages to deliver, lives to change and protect. You need to stop being selfish and remember your path." She scolded.

I hung my head, looking at the grass as its brightness faded in the dwindling sunlight. "You are right. I haven't known what I was doing this past year. At this time last year. I was running all over New Orleans telling people messages from loved ones that have passed on. What has happened to me?" I lifted my eyes to look at her.

She softened her gaze and looked down at me. "Have you really tried to be still and listen for God's white light to guide you?"

"I tried, then the cardinal totally distracted me. When the sounds of nature call and I don't hear Him."

"No, He spoke to you to bring you here. Keep trying, He'll tell you more."

"What does 'let your light shine' mean? People keep saying it to me."

"I don't know the specifics. I just deliver the message. Don't you let people figure out what their messages mean to them?"

"Yeah, I guess you are right," I said, searching my brain thinking back to the messages I've delivered. I learned key images that would help me deliver the message to them from their loved ones, but most of the time it was up to the individual to figure out the deeper message.

"Remember the time you shared with the lady with the brown derby hat?" She displayed the memory before us by opening her hands wide facing the sky. A light flickered and showed a tan woman with a brown derby hat. She wore a yellow dress with little blue flowers. Her face was swollen from tears that had fallen just moments before. She closed her eyes hard, deep in thought. I heard what sounded like my voice, but a little higher octave than I thought I should sound like. I leaned in to watch closer, reliving the memory from the outside.

"Excuse me," I greeted the woman. Her eyes popped open and she looked at me, but didn't say anything. "I'm sorry to bother you, I can see you suffered something tragic, and I don't mean to deepen any possible wounds." She folded her arms and wrapped her hands around her torso, hugging herself still not speaking to me.

"I want to tell you that your daughter did not suffer." Nervously I put my hand over my mouth and continued to speak. The woman put her fingers inside my hand almost touching my lips and pulled my hand away from my mouth watching my lips. She caused me to pause. Still not speaking, she rolled her hand in a motion as if to say, continue.

"Okay," I said, blinking, still startled by her touching me. "Your daughter said she did not suffer, and she is in God's glory and waits for you to be reunited."

A solid line of tears streamed down her face as she shuttered and tried to breathe. She dropped her head and placed her hand on my shoulder.

"There's more." The vibration of my voice caused her to lift her head and quickly wipe her eyes trying to focus on me. She tapped me on the shoulder and held up an index finger to tell me to wait. Taking the white handkerchief from her dress pocket completely dried her eyes. Blinking rapidly, she composed herself with as dry eyes as possible and ran her hand in a circle once again telling me to continue.

"There's more," I said starting over, "you will have a new baby. Your daughter said, name her, Renata, it means born again."

The woman shook, holding back her tears, but they couldn't be contained. She draped her arms around me wetting my shoulder with

184

tears. She pulled me back and finally spoke, "Thank you." Her speech revealed to me that she was hearing impaired.

Crystal closed her hand and the vision disappeared into the darkness. She said, "That's what you could be doing."

I admitted, "I really miss being able to do that. Ever since the battle with Miranda LaTour things have changed. She didn't take my powers, but they seemed to become stronger."

"You may be stronger, but you don't seem any smarter," Crystal said plainly to me.

"This doesn't explain being the light either." I pointed it out to her. Glancing around I saw the sun was setting fast. I wasn't sure if I could make it home in time. The clouds continued to flow quickly in the sky. The trees blocked out the little bit of sunshine that was left. I sure lost track of time. Should I stay in the cemetery for the night or try to venture in the dark back to the plantation? Stupidly I didn't tell anyone where I was going. I know by now they figured out I was either lost or at least missing for dinner. I asked Crystal "Can I stay here for the night safely?"

She told me, "I cannot leave the cemetery, so I can only protect you within the gates."

The sounds of the night started to roll in with songs of the crickets. Birds drifted home to nestle in for the night calling to each other as if to say, it was a good day, see you tomorrow and we will do it again. The trees rustled from the breeze that blew all around us. Small animals crunched on the fallen twigs around the perimeter of the cemetery.

The cardinal flew to me hovering above, peeping at me before he took off into the dusky sky. I guess even he didn't want to be away from home for the night. The moon started to rise. Thankfully it was almost completely full, casting a nice glow on my surroundings. The clouds turned to grey puffs in the fading blue sky. There was a hint of pink saying goodbye to the sun. I watched the clouds glide away and disappear behind the trees around the cemetery. The winds picked up and died down frequently.

"I guess I'll stay here." I shivered from the cool of the night. There was a little rumble in the distance warning me that rain was nearby. I wrapped my arms around myself trying to keep my body heat from dropping. It could get down into the forties tonight, I was thankful it was still a warm winter.

Crystal picked me up and brought me up on top of the tomb where she had been living for all this time. I sat with my legs folded trying to look out into the night for any signs of life. Bushes shuffled as animals moved around doing their nightly stuff. I couldn't see what animals were out there, but they were moving around. The sounds of raindrops started to patter as they hit the ground releasing the musky smell of the earth to fill my nose. Crystal tapped on the white pedestal with the palm of her hand three times. The side panel of the tomb made a grinding sound of cement rubbing on cement as it opened to reveal the inside of the tomb was empty.

Lowering me down to the ground level she said, "Climb in and you will stay dry and warm for the night."

I cautiously put my right foot inside and stooped down to enter. Once inside the interior was not comparable to the outside. I could stand straight up and not hit the ceiling, but from the outside I would have to curl up to really fit inside. Laying on my side I faced the outside world. I could see her delicate hand drape in front of the opening to keep me protected inside. Allowing myself to relax and feel safe, I drifted off to sleep.

Sounds in the distance caused my eyes to flutter open allowing me to see the rain had stopped and the lightning was gone. A beam of light flashed and I caught a glimpse of an angel gliding by with a long sword. I got up and climbed out of the tomb. The moon had shifted, and it was dark over the cemetery.

I called into the night, "Who's out there?"

Turning back to the tomb I saw the opening was sealed shut. Pulling myself to the top of the tomb I touched her wing, "Crystal are you there?" Her body was draped across her pedestal with her head down resting on her right wrist. Her left arm hung down over the edge, just like what I saw from the inside before. Her wings draped down beside her. I looked at her wavy hair, noticing her flower headpiece was missing. She looked as if she was resting.

186

"Thank you for waiting for me." I said to Crystal. Her wings fluttered slightly and froze again.

"Arielle!"

I turned to be blinded by a flashlight. Holding my hands over my eyes I asked, "Charlie? Is that you?"

"How'd you get way out here?" He asked with a tone of anger.

"I followed a bird."

"Okay, Snow White, let's get you home." He softened his voice.

"The bird was red, not blue like Snow White's," I tried to joke.

"Too soon." He said, "You're smarter than this. Something could have happened to you. Don't you know there are wolves and coyotes out here?"

"I left when it was daylight. Anyway, Crystal protected me." I said pointing to the resting angel next to me.

"She looks like she is sleeping on the job," he said.

"She has feelings, don't pick on her," I said from experience.

Charlie squeezed his lips thin keeping his comment to himself. "You ready to head back?"

I turned to look at Crystal who was not moving from her new position. "Yes, I think my time here's over." I climbed off the tomb to meet Charlie.

He pulled a second flashlight out of his cargo pocket and handed it to me to keep the path lit in front of us. Charlie took my hand and led me into the dark night. It took several hours to make our way back to the grounds. It was not the same path either. I didn't see the large tree that I had to climb over and slide down. He had to release my hand a few times to pull back vines and branches that filled the makeshift path. In the far distance I could see lights from the house. The trees started to be less dense showing the sky. I glanced up to see the clouds were gone and the moon was visible from where we were.

The cardinal buzzed by peeping at us. I pointed with the flashlight, "There he is!"

Charlie asked, "Why didn't you just follow him back to the house then?"

"He left before I was ready," I said smartly.

"Come on, we're almost home. I am exhausted from searching for you."

"I'm sorry. Thank you for coming for me."

"You're welcome. No supper for you, the house is all asleep."

"Did Ms. LuLu help you find me?" I quizzed him.

"Yes, she showed me you were at the old cemetery. I just didn't remember how to get to it since it is not on our property. I saw you were safe, but I couldn't leave you there all night."

"I needed to talk to Crystal. She helped me find my path again. I need to get back to the city and just start giving people their messages again."

"What about Aunt Nina's book?"

"I'm tired of forcing stuff, it'll come when it is supposed to."

"But Ms. LuLu and I were going to help you find it," Charlie said.

"Maybe I'm not supposed to find it right now? I'm going to spend time reading Papa's book learning what I can and getting back to what I do know. Spreading messages to others from their loved ones. And planning a wedding!"

"Okay, Arielle. But for now, let's get some sleep?"

"Deal."

CHAPTER TWENTY-ONE

Back to the Basics

After a cup of coffee, and a plate of scrambled eggs, grits and butter, Charlie picked up our plates and said, "Go find Ms. LuLu in the garden. She wants to talk to you before we leave."

"Do you want me to help clean up the kitchen?" I asked standing.

Charlie said pointing in the direction of the kitchen, "Go out the side door; she is waiting for you."

Sunshine streamed between the chunky white clouds creating a hazy glow. A small yellow butterfly bounced along in front of me chasing another yellow butterfly. They swirled and danced together heading to the garden. I walked, watching them land on a tall stalk. I noticed that the garden remained green even with the falling leaves and dying grass around. A pink and purple tinted bubble drifted from the center of the garden.

"Ms. LuLu?" I called, "You wanted to see me?"

"Come on in," she called from behind rows of thick green stalks.

Picking a row, I parted the leaves making my way toward her. Looking up I followed the few bubbles in the sky leading me to her location. We met by the tomato bushes. They were so tall it loomed above us casting shadows.

"I found you," I said to her.

"What gave me away?" she said, gently flicking bubbles in my direction.

I laughed, catching a bubble as it popped in my palm. "I think you already know that I am not going to hunt for Mr. Wolf."

She nodded, lifting the leaf so I could see her better. "Yes, I know, and I understand."

"Thank you for understanding. I need to go back to my roots where this all started. The battles, the fighting, is just not me."

"I can see that," she said, creating a large iridescent bubble in her hand like a crystal ball. She held it up between us, releasing it into the air. We both gazed into it. Inside we saw Mr. Wolf holding Aunt Nina's book, pulling on it with his hairy hands. He shook the book, tossing it hard onto the ground. He picked it up, prying his fingers into the pages and tried to pull it apart again. Taking the corner of the book he put it in between his teeth and bit. The bubble popped and the vision disappeared.

"I also see wedding bells." said Ms. LuLu

I twisted the oval opal ring to examine it again closely. I smiled. "I'm excited, but still not sure what life will hold for us. Where are we going to live?" I asked, meeting eyes with Ms. LuLu.

"Dear one, God will provide for you," she assured me.

"Yes, you are right." I agreed with her finding peace in her words.

"There's something I'd like to ask you to do for me."

"Me, help you?" I asked with my eyebrows furrowed trying to figure out what I could do for her. "Absolutely, what is it?"

"Charlie." She smiled gently at me.

"Charlie?" I asked.

"I have known him all his life. There is a spark of something special with him too. Can you try to talk to him about it? I don't want him to waste it by never trying to figure it out."

"I'll try," I promised her.

Heading back into town I began to uphold my promise to Ms. LuLu, "Charlie, don't you think you have something special to offer. Ms. LuLu thinks you have something you need to explore. You could stay here and develop it, maybe together we could make even a bigger difference for the people in our community? Who knows what you are capable of? I'm still learning what my gifts are, imagine the two of us together."

190

Waiting for his response my mind wandered. *Oh, imagine if our children could have even more powers if you have something inside of you too!*

I continued, "I know it's scary trying to figure out what it is and what if you misinterpret it? But you don't know if you don't try. Why not explore together? Everyone keeps telling me to 'Be still and let your light shine.' Have you tried to be still?" I paused again, giving him a chance to respond. He remained silent.

"I'm still trying to figure out what God is saying to me. I get messages to pass onto others, but I sometimes miss the direct message for myself and my path. Do you want me to be still and ask for you? Have you ever been in danger and seen something that might help you get out of it? It could be that kind of power. Or maybe you can pass messages too? I have not met anyone who has the same gift as myself yet. Maybe we all have different gifts for a reason so we can come together for the greater good of God passing His word on to others. I mean the whole reason we are here is to be disciples of His word, right?"

Finally, he said, "Yes that part is true, we're all here to pass on His word."

"Is that all I'm going to get from you?" I asked with an annoyed tone in my voice.

"Yes, that's all you will get from me right now. I'm listening to you if that matters."

"I suppose that's something." I sat in the jeep with my arms folded trying to not be annoyed that he didn't want to jump right in and discuss this with me.

Charlie pulled his Jeep onto the sidewalk in front of my home leaving the engine running. He slid out and came to the passenger door. It creaked open and I stepped out. Charlie wrapped his arms around me as I stood there with my arms crossed not hugging him back. "I just want to help you. Why won't you let me?" I asked in a low tone.

"I will, but I don't see what you see. Or Ms. LuLu for that matter," he admitted.

"Okay. At least you're giving me some hope."

"Don't give up on me Arielle." He pulled back and winked at me still holding my shoulders.

"Ugh," I said with a small chuckle and shifted my eyes. *I can't stay mad at him,* I thought to myself.

He lifted my chin with his curled index finger lifting my lips to his. All my annoyance melted away with the soft kiss.

"When are you coming back?" I asked.

Lifting his eyes in thought. "Today is Tuesday. I have some things to tend to at the alligator farm, but I'll come back on Friday and stay the weekend. How does that sound?" he asked.

"I want you to stay longer, but I'll be happy to spend the weekend with you."

"Be safe."

"As best as I can, I will." I promised. I stood leaning against the side of the house until he turned down the end of the road.

I glanced around trying to locate the demon's hiding and waiting to see where I will go and who I will speak to. They breathed deeply. I could hear them creeping around. I ignore them as the tingling feeling appears on the middle of my forehead. I breathe in and ask for God's white light to come to me, bless me for the ability to hear and deliver the messages I am given.

Here I go, I thought to myself as I walked down the uneven brick sidewalk. Searching for the person He wants me to talk to, I watched a bald man with a black t-shirt roll a trash can out of the restaurant parking lot in front of me. I took in the sounds, smells, and visions He placed before me. I halted and waited. He didn't see me as I focused on him trying to see if there is a message he needs to hear.

Something gently urges me to continue as I glide past him unnoticed. *Nope, it isn't him* I thought to myself. I keep walking down the sidewalk turning my head looking at each person I see. It isn't anyone on the street. My forehead tingles stronger. I rub my index finger down the middle trying to get it to lighten up a little. It never works, but

I always try. Standing on the corner of St. Peter and Chartres Street I then continued down St. Peter Street where something catches my eye.

The Gumbo Pot restaurant's main entrance glowed a soft yellow as if the sun was setting inside the building. *Well, if that isn't a sign, I don't know what is?!* I thought to myself as I stepped into the street without looking. A long honk snapped me back to reality! I put both hands out low, shake them and mouth, "Sorry!" backing up on the curb.

The angry driver raises his hands above his head yelling at me, "What are you doing? Damn tourist, pay attention!" I pushed my bottom lip to the side and opened my eyes wide, giving him a little shrug.

Back on the curb and extending my hand, saying, "After you."

He shook his head with his eyebrows so annoyed it looks like he has one giant fuzzy caterpillar. He squished his lips into a pucker and pulled away leaving me. I glanced toward the Gumbo Pot. The front door still glowed a beautiful sunset color inviting me to come visit.

This was a very busy intersection. I waited as the cars constantly pulled through. Finally, after the seventh car I had a break. The car next to me with a stop sign peeled out tired of waiting for the traffic to die down. Once he was clear, I bolted to the other side. I put my face against the window with hands cupped around my eyes, peeking in to see how many people were inside. The wait staff leaned against the bar along the back of the small establishment.

No one noticed me looking in because they were chattering to each other. It was around 3 pm, not a prime time for lunch or dinner, especially on a Tuesday. At least it wasn't Monday, or I would have found the Gumbo Pot closed.

I gave a pull on the brass handle that was worn in the middle. The sunset color that had been the beacon that drew me to this location had dimmed to the yellow light of the old lightbulbs hanging overhead.

A woman in black hustled over to me, "How many?"

"Just one."

Her shoulders dropped, hoping it would be a larger group to make the time pass. She pulled a menu from under the hostess stand and said, "Follow me." She placed me at a window seat for two. I fixed my eyes on the back of her shiny black hair as she took me to my table. Nope it wasn't her either. I sat down and picked up the menu she slapped down on the chair she assigned me. A woman came over with her notepad in hand, "What will you have to drink?"

"Water with lemon?" I said, staring at her while she started to write then stopped realizing that it wouldn't cost me anything and no reason to record it. "Are you waiting for anyone else?" she asked obviously not looking that there was only one menu on the table.

I raised the menu, "Just me."

She walked away. *Great, I get to tell a sour puss a message,* I thought to myself. I tried to remember the way I treated Crystal the angel. The waitress came back and placed the water and two small squares of ice floated on the top with no lemons.

"Can I have some lemons?" I asked.

She didn't even respond, just walked away. I studied the menu, losing my appetite, but I still had to tell her something. I just didn't know what yet. She came back and slid the small white bowl with one lemon in it.

Smiling at her, "What do you recommend?" I asked, trying to get her to lighten up a little.

"Are you from here?" she asked.

"Yes, I live not too far from here, just never been here before."

"Then you should know everything is good," she said with her one brow raised in annoyance.

"Have you had the seafood gumbo?"

"Yes, it's good," she said numbly.

"What about the shrimp creole?"

"Yes, it's good," she said almost like a recording.

I tried to be cheerful, but she wasn't interested in making nice. I guessed she figured I was young enough to not have money to tip well so why treat me well. A vision flashed of a man in a pinstripe suit. That wasn't enough to get a conversation started.

"I will start with the seafood gumbo, I don't know what else I want yet."

She snapped her notepad shut without writing anything down and turned on her heels walking back to the bar. I watched her, she didn't even put my order in. She chatted and laughed with a coworker and then slapped her hand on the bar letting out a huge belly laugh. Then meandered to the kitchen. I thought, *What a turd! Why God do you want me to bless her? She doesn't deserve it. You wanted me to get back into this message delivering why are You making it difficult for me?*

As I waited, I played with the empty white bowl. She didn't even bring me a straw and didn't come back for me to ask.

The light flickered several times in the restaurant. My vision changed and I was transported to a school room. The paint on the walls was chipping around the window unit that dripped on the typical square off-white and black flecked classroom tiles. The room smelled like mold from the water leak. I stood next to a wall entirely of windows Examining them I assumed the custodian had painted them shut to prevent them from being opened.

A loud buzzer sounded over the intercom, kids flooded in and chattered loudly, most of them taking their seats. A boy grabbed a sandy blond girl's hair tugging on it. She slapped him and gave him a shove. He stumbled back and laughed at her. I didn't recognize any of the kids.

The teacher with a tight salt and pepper bun came in and hollered for the kids to quiet down. They were going to take a pop quiz so they should get their pencils out. A groan waved across the classroom. She quieted them by saying, "keep it up and there will be two pop quizzes." She emphasized the two by flicking her right hand holding out two fingers. Not wanting to call her bluff, they all stopped in their tracks.

Making her way up and down the aisles her long denim jumper dress brushed along the desks. She shifted her eyes on each kid watching as they jotted down their answer to the history questions. The same boy leaned over to the girl and tried to look at her paper. She slapped his pencil out of his hand and it clinked onto the floor. She giggled quietly but her shoulder shook, giving her away.

The teacher called her to stand up. "What's going on over there?"

"He's cheating!" she said with her voice reaching a high pitch sound, pointing at the boy who was trying to pick up his pencil between them.

"Okay, both of you go to the office and you can let the principal figure this out." The teacher shoved them toward the hallway door.

The girl's mouth gaped open and said, "But I'm not cheating. He is!"

"I don't care and that's not for me to figure out. You can have Principal Peterson decide that. Both of you, off."

The girl crossed her arms and stomped out of the classroom. The boy hung his head and followed behind her. I followed them undetected in my vision, down the hallway listening to them.

"What's the big deal anyway? It's just a pop quiz," he said out of the corner of his mouth to the girl.

"You're not going to cheat off me," she quipped.

"Why would you turn me in?"

"Teach you a lesson."

"What a great lesson, you're in trouble now too," he pointed out.

"Whatever dude. Don't talk to me," the sandy blonde girl said to him.

They walked into the office and the secretary said to the boy, "What did you do now, Steve?"

"Nothing."

"That isn't what Mrs. Barrilleaux said when she buzzed the office."

"Oh. Well, she said it wasn't for her to decide so maybe she was confused?" Steve said with a shrug.

196

"And you, young lady, what are you doing letting him cheat?" the secretary asked.

"I didn't. I swear." she wailed.

"It takes two to cheat," the secretary remarked. "Principal Peterson is in a meeting, y'all take a seat."

A woman came out of the office ringing her hands. I watched her sit next to the kids. Her eyes were red and puffy from tears. The secretary scurried into his office to report about the two cheaters.

The principal peeked his head out and glanced at the kids then back to the woman. "I'm so sorry for your loss. Please let us know if we can do anything." He turned to the kids, "You guys are in big trouble, just wait." He closed his door as the secretary took her seat behind the counter.

The woman rose and asked, "Could you please call Elizabeth Lewis?" The secretary nodded with a sad face. She pressed a button and a sound buzzed in a classroom far away.

"Ms. Thieme, could you please send Elizabeth to the front office?"

She answered, "Yes, she's on her way."

The principal never came out. I waited to see what would develop next. A teenager came into the office. My mouth formed a small 'O' as I saw the dark long hair, tiny, pointed nose, and scattered freckles across her cheeks. She is my waitress! This was why I didn't recognize the kids in the classroom. I was supposed to come to the office. *Good thing those brats got in trouble,* I thought to myself.

The woman tried to hide her eyes behind sunglasses, but her red nose gave it away she had been crying. She put her hand out and Elizabeth took it, they went into the hallway for privacy, I followed.

"Elizabeth, your daddy was hurt at work today on the oil rig," her mom told her gently and quietly.

"Is he going to be okay?" she asked with wrinkles in her forehead of concern.

"No baby, he isn't going to be okay," she admitted.

The teenager stood there blinking in disbelief as her mom wrapped her arms around her and held her tight. "We're going to be okay, Elizabeth, I promise."

I watched the young girl's face crumble, she was about 16 years old, but her grief aged her almost instantly. She was transformed into her current age, and I was brought back to current time.

She stood in front of me. "Hello?" she asked with annoyance trying to get my attention. "Are you going to order anything else?"

"Maybe. Can I have my gumbo first?" trying to get her away from the table so I could figure out what God wanted me to do with this old information.

She rolled her eyes and walked off. "Sure."

I knew she lost her dad in an oil rig disaster when she was a teenager. I know he was wearing a pinstripe suit. But what else?

She brought the bowl plopping it down loudly in front of me and walked off abruptly.

"Thanks," I mumbled. I folded my hand and thanked God for my food and that I had a spoon! I asked for guidance and information.

I slowly spooned the gumbo into my mouth enjoying the warm dark roux and chunks of seafood. I looked at the menu trying to find something else to order. I decided on the fried catfish platter. *No way I could eat it all, but I could bring it home,* I thought.

She sauntered back over, "Well, you decide?" she asked with her hand extended to take the menu fully expecting me to not order anything else.

"Yes, catfish platter, please," I said, putting the menu squarely in her hand. "Why are you so grumpy? You should be nicer if you are working in service." The words just slipped out.

She held the menu to her chest and her mouth gaped open, "Psh." She pushed air out and rolled her eyes. "Whatever, kid," she muttered and walked away.

I hope they don't spit in my food, I thought.

She dropped the menu off at the hostess stand and went back over to her friend that worked at the bar. They talked and she pointed at me as if telling her friend how dare she say that she was grumpy. They both glanced at me, turning away when they saw I was watching them while eating my gumbo. She left and went into the kitchen. I waited for her to come back. The bartender came by and picked up my empty gumbo bowl.

"Where's my waitress?" I asked him.

"She left."

"Why?"

"The owner heard you and sent her home. Thanks a lot. She needed the money," he whispered to me so no one would hear him.

"Can I get my food to go?" I had lost my appetite.

"Yep," the bartender said and came back very quickly with a white Styrofoam box and a bill on top of the box. "Whenever you're ready."

"I'm ready, I pulled cash from my pocket and put a twenty on the bill.

He went to the bar to cash out the check. When he came back with my change and put it on the table.

I asked, "Can you make sure she gets her tip?"

"Yes," He paused to say something else, but turned and left instead.

I walked home in the shadows as the sun was starting to drop down lower. Carrying my box of food, I still had a tingling feeling in my forehead because I didn't get to complete the task. I put the food in the fridge in case Mama would want them tomorrow. I trudged upstairs. That was not what I was expecting at all. I was all recharged to make a difference and all I did was make a mess.

Standing in the shower I rinsed the day from my body and scrubbed my face. After drying off I put on my PJs and slipped on fuzzy socks. Climbing out onto the second story escape platform in our house,

I sat and looked up at the sky. Mark, my older brother and I used to sit up here and talk for hours to escape the chaos of the house.

Mama and Papa had a lot of foster kids in our home growing up. Mama wanted to help the kids that needed direction. She found her passion in high school students that were lost and needed guidance. At one point we had as many as twelve kids - not including us - in our home. Everyone had their position or chore to make the house run smoothly. Most of the teenagers were happy to be here and Mama made sure to connect with each one giving them love and attention.

Sometimes I felt annoyed that I didn't have her full attention growing up but looking at the transformation in the kids I understood why she did it. After Papa died, she stopped her mission. It has been a few years and even with a cancer scare and finding out she would be okay, she still had not resumed fostering teenagers.

Papa was her rock, so without him I didn't know if she ever will have them in our home again. She spent last summer in Michigan visiting family. She went again for New Years and Mari Gras. She said, "I don't want to have to deal with all the drunken tourists." I understood since our home was an attraction due to the history of this house.

I hope she finds her way back to her passion. There was a lot that needed her, hell, I still needed her! It was nice to have her back home tomorrow especially since we were going wedding dress shopping with Dixie and her mom. The wedding was in two weeks.

I told Mama over the phone a few days ago, "Dixie is getting married before her belly starts to show. You need to come home." In one quick sentence I revealed why I stayed back. Mama changed her flight to come home earlier than she planned.

Watching the far away stars twinkle in the sky I asked, "Okay God, what am I supposed to do with this waitress?" I closed my eyes and breathed in the cold night air causing me to cough a little. I listened to the sounds of the people milling around the street. A far away band played at a nightclub. I can't be still with all this chatter. I was shivering from the cold and went back into my room. I sat on the floor and ran my fingers through the rug that surrounded my bed. Be still, I told myself.

Giving up, I took out Papa's book for a little reading. I opened it and the pages flipped, searching for where it wanted to stop. The page landed and I put my right hand on the right page and tried to read the left page. The room was too dark. There was not enough light from my little stained-glass lamp. Papa's book started to glow providing enough light to read. The ceiling fan was lightly tossing my hair as I read.

'Things are hard right now. I am trying to steady the course. Money is tight, but I know God will provide. He always has and always will. More than just money, things are moving faster with Kaye and me. Our blind date was perfect except for the uninvited visitors. Sometimes I wish I could just turn it off and have a normal life. She is so much shorter than I am, but I love the smell of her shampoo when we dance in each other's arms. Her soft curly brown head fits perfectly in my chest.'

Wiping away the tear that stopped on my cheek I let out a huge sigh and went back to reading.

'I feel she is my soulmate. She makes me want to be a better man. I haven't told her about my secret. I can see souls of the dead. They are all different glowing colors and sizes. I know they are trying to speak to me. I don't know if I will need to share this with her.'

I wondered to myself; Did Mama ever know about Papa? It seems like he was able to save her from the heartache, but then she also missed out on the joyous parts as well. The pages flipped quickly moving to a story toward the end of the book.

'Breakthrough: I heard one of the souls today! It was a man who was working on an oil rig and was in an accident.'

My heart dropped as I considered that my Papa might be writing about the father of Elizabeth, the waitress.

'He had a wife and a daughter that he left behind. It makes me think about my wife, Kaye, and kiddos Mark and Arielle. He didn't get to say goodbye. He wants me to find his family and tell them about the insurance policy. I can't find them. I don't know how to find them, but this is the policy number in case I do. Policy No. 6412731 with the Benoit Company.'

Gently closing the book, I flopped down in the bed. "I have to find Elizabeth!"

Mama is flying in around noon tomorrow and we are due to meet at the dress shop, House of Brulé at, 2 pm. I hope I can make it all work to get this nagging feeling to go away. For now, I will try to get some rest.

CHAPTER TWENTY-TWO
Madame Brule

My eyes popped open. I quickly showered and slapped on some mascara and lipstick and jogged downstairs to head to the restaurant to look for Elizabeth. It was around 8 am and the morning crew was shuffling in, still bleary eyed from their late evening. There she was coming up the street. She didn't look up until I called her name, "Elizabeth!"

"Oh my god, what do you want?" she glared.

"Please, just hear me out," I pleaded.

"I don't have time for your crap. I already lost a night's wage because of you."

"Seriously," I grabbed her wrist and a jolt of electricity pulsed from me shocking her.

"Get your hands off me, crazy!" She pulled away trying to get around me to go into the restaurant.

"I'm serious, you'll listen to me." I commanded. I normally took a softer approach when giving messages. I was a little rusty and frankly still annoyed at her rudeness from yesterday too. "Look, give me 5 minutes and you never have to see me again."

"Don't touch me again." she warned me, pointing a finger close to my nose. She cupped her hand around the lighter and the end of the cigarette that dangled from her red lips.

"I won't, but you have to listen to everything I tell you," I challenged her.

"How do you know my name anyway? Are you stalking me?" Elizabeth asked, pushing out a long cloud of smoke and flicking the ash on the sidewalk.

"Not exactly, I can speak to the dead."

"Oh no, I'm not listening to this crap, get out of my way," she returned the cigarette to her lips and tried to push around me.

"No, you have to give me 5 mins," I held my arms out to stop her.

"Fine, but you have wasted one already," she smirked and blew smoke over my head.

"Your dad had an insurance policy that you and your mom didn't know about." Taking a quick breath, I rushed to continue, "I have the number and the company." I held out a small, folded piece of paper.

"You are not funny," she stood with her arms crossed flicking the rest of her cigarette on the sidewalk and pressed down twisting with the ball of her boot.

"I know I'm not funny, and I would never joke about the dead. You don't know me, so why should you trust me, but what could it hurt?" I asked. "Take it," I said, thrusting the paper toward her.

She snatched it and opened it, folded it back in half and raised it up next to her head and asked me. "Really, this is just some number and a company scribbled on notebook paper. What do you expect me to do with this?"

"Call them and ask, what could it hurt?"

She rolled her eyes and shoved the paper in her black work pants, "Fine. We done now?"

I moved toward the street side and let her pass toward the door, "Thank you for the 5 minutes."

"Sure," she said, waving her hand, dismissing me.

Scratching my forehead lightly with my fingernail, I waited. The tingling feeling was gone. A huge smile filled my face as I thought, *That wasn't quite the same, but at least it is done. Good job, Arielle. I even have time to go home and relax before Mama gets home.*

****

Mama, Ms. DeeDee, and I sat on the plush pink chairs waiting for Dixie to come out with the last of the 12 dresses we picked out. Clutching the cloth in both hands she stepped up on the round pedestal surrounded by three full length mirrors. She released the dress and the intricate lace flowed. Slowly she looked at us for approval. Her cheeks rounded from her smile as tears formed in the corners of her eyes.

"You look beautiful," Mama said.

"Do you like it, Dixie?" asked Ms. DeeDee. "You look like a fresh lily. I love it." She told her daughter as she touched the corner of her eyes with her small handkerchief.

"Well?" she turned to ask me.

"I think we have a winner! You look perfect," I told her.

"Well almost," the owner said as she tucked the comb of the veil at the top of her head. The veil flowed down Dixie's exposed shoulders and back. "Now it is complete."

Dixie took one side of her dress raising it. She made a small curtsy and we all applauded in approval.

"What's next on the agenda?" I asked Dixie.

Counting on her fingers. "Venue, check. Cake, check. Invites ordered, check. Bridesmaids' dresses, check. My dress, big check!" she said, making a check mark with her index finger in the air. "I think that's about it."

"You got that done in record time," I commended her.

She rested her hand on her stomach and gave a side smile at me and raised eyebrows. I nodded and smiled. Her and Ernie's wedding was scheduled only two weeks from today. Not wanting her belly to show any more than needed, they chose to move forward swiftly. The seamstress walked between Dixie and I ending our silent conversation. They began to chatter about length, taking in a few areas and such things. I turned to face our moms who were catching up since Mama had been out of town.

I whispered to them, "I will be right back. I have to potty."

They smiled, nodded at me and continued their conversation. I found a small bathroom under the staircase. Tossing the paper towel in the wastepaper basket I glanced in the mirror to fluff my hair a bit before rejoining the gals. Voices echoed above me on the stairs and laughter filled the air. I smiled at the infectious laughter rounding the bend. I looked up the stairs to see who it was. The staircase was empty, but the laughter continued. Hypnotized by such joy I followed the giggles. I found myself at the top of the stairs peeking into different rooms finding them empty. I made a circle again, looking, never finding anyone. Pausing at the top of the staircase a woman's voice called to me from the bottom. "Did you find the bathroom, my dear?"

"Oh yes Ma'am. I'm sorry, I thought I heard something," I responded as I walked back down the stairs.

"Laughter perhaps?" the owner suggested.

"Yes," I admitted on the last step to the ground level.

"They must like you," she said, wrapping her arm around my waist giving me a squeeze.

"They?" I tried to be as nonchalant as possible.

"The spirits who live here," she said point blankly. "What's your gift?" she asked.

I paused really thinking about how to answer this question. "Well, I'm trying to figure out some new things, but I used to give messages from those who have passed on." After being quick to share I thought *What am I doing? This lady is going to think I'm crazy! I shouldn't be talking to her. I don't know anything about her.*

"That is a very special gift," she released me and smiled gently. "Would you like a cup of tea?" she asked me.

I shifted my weight to my other leg holding my elbow with my arm crossed across my waist trying to not look uncomfortable. "I really should be getting back. My friend is getting her dress altered."

"You have already helped her with the hardest part, picking the right dress."

Looking up and then to the left thinking about what she said and not wanting to be rude I responded, "True. I am sure they won't miss me while I have a quick cup of tea." I followed her toward the back of the house into a small kitchen area. She motioned to a chair.

"Earl Grey?" she asked me.

"Sounds great, thank you. Do you need help with anything?" I asked.

She placed the tea kettle on the gas stove and said, "No thank you."

I crossed my legs then uncrossed them. Spreading my navy plaid skirt to make sure I looked presentable and crossed my legs at my ankles. *Good enough. Stop freaking out Arielle.* Coming back, she placed two delicate teacups with saucers on the small table and went to fetch a small matching pourer with cream. The kettle called for attention as she glided to turn off the heat. The pot was placed on a trivet in the center of the table. She put a small tin next to it. When my eyes fell on the golden tin a small tear formed. It was exactly the same box that Aunt Nina had. I watched the woman open the tin box and scoop out the Earl Grey tea leaves, placing them in a small silver ball and locking the leaves in. She plopped it in the teacup. Then poured the hot water over the leaves. I tapped the side of my eye to dry the small tear as she continued to do the same for her cup.

"Thank you." I bounced the ball in the hot water changing the color to a light brown color.

"You're welcome, my dear," she said, doing the same to her teacup. "Sugar or cream?"

"Two lumps and cream, please." I responded while taking the silver ball out to examine the color of the tea. Satisfied with the honey color, I placed the silver ball on my saucer. Dropping one of the sugar cubes from the sterling silver claws into my cup, I added one more. Swirling the sugar to dissolve it, my cup pulsed a maroon light once. I quickly glanced at the woman. She smiled softly. Looking back at my cup I wondered if she too saw the maroon light.

She tapped her spoon lightly and placed it on her saucer, "So tell me a little about yourself."

Pouring a little cream in my tea, I stirred again. "I have lived here all my life. My mama is Kaye Mathis and my papa Denny passed away a few years ago. I was going to college, but I am not sure if that is right for me." I paused for a sip, and she picked up the silence.

"I remember your father. Very kind man. He had a special gift as well," she said, taking a sip and looking at my response over the rim of the dainty cup.

"I'm still learning about him even though he isn't here to teach me directly," I admitted, smiling.

"We're all students of this world, and the next. There's much to learn about both."

"I'm searching for my next mentor," I told her, locking eyes.

"I'm searching for my next mentee," she whispered. "Maybe we are a good fit?"

I shuttered a deep breath and a stream of tears cut down my cheeks. "That would be amazing."

"Funny how God will place the right person in your path when He knows you need it the most. Just remember to be still and listen to him."

"He has been telling me that and to let my light shine," I added.

"How are you doing with that?"

"Not very well," I admitted.

"I guess I should properly introduce myself," she extended her hand to me, holding back her flowing sleeve from draping across the small table. "My name's Madame Brulé."

I took her hand and my vision blurred. I saw large puffy clouds zoom by my eyes. Giving me a small glimpse of the room where she was sitting across from me. The clouds chopped the view like an old movie reel. All I could see was white as the clouds moved faster and faster. I spun in a circle coming back to her surrounded in white. "Where are we?" I asked.

"This is my gift," she extended her arms showing the pureness around us.

208

"I don't understand," I said perplexed, with my eyebrows scrunched.

"It takes a while to get the hang of it," she comforted me. "Close your eyes," she said, waving her hand across my face. I followed her hand from above my forehead down, closing my eyes. She whispered, "Now take a deep breath and hold it for six seconds and release it."

"Can I open my eyes?" I asked.

"If you have to ask, then you are not ready to see," she calmly explained. "Why don't you try to clear your mind."

With my eyes wrinkled tight, I felt for the ground and sat down with my legs crossed placing my hands on my bent knees.

"Try to relax."

"I really should get back to Dixie," I said, fighting the need to relax.

"Lucky for you time is frozen while you are here, just another perk of my gift," she chuckled lightly.

I guess I'm not getting out of this anytime soon. Arielle, just relax! I said to myself.

"Try breathing the same way a few times."

"Okay, I'll try." I repeated the pattern of breathing and let my mind empty from all the chatter going on. Madame Brulé didn't utter a word while I tried to be still. I lost count of how many times I held my breath after around nine. I wanted to ask if I could open my eyes again, but I remembered she had already answered that question.

My body started to feel a warmth like the sun was shining the top of my head. I lifted my face with my eyes still closed. I could see the brightness beyond my eyelids. I needed to open my eyes and see the light. I didn't ask this time. I rounded my shoulders and dropped them into complete relaxation. The tension in my face melted away as my eyes fluttered open to the most glorious sight. White puffy clouds took shape forming a man. As the monotone man walked toward me little flashes of color pinged out of the clouds touching him, filling in flesh

209

tones, coloring his hair, down to coloring his charcoal pinstripe suit. As he approached, my smile grew. "Hi Charlie," I said softly.

"Hi Arielle, this is our first dance as a married couple, will you join me?" He bowed slightly at the waist and extended his hand to mine.

"I would love to."

He gently spun me around and pulled me close to him. *Is this real? He sure feels real.* I thought to myself.

"We have been through a lot, haven't we?" he asked me.

"Yes, but goodness always prevails, right?" I responded.

"God's will be done. Have you found your path?" he asked softly in my ear.

"I found you," I said.

"You're on your journey, but there's more." He spun me around and was gone.

I stumbled a little looking around for anyone. I was alone. Sitting down again, I started to breathe the pattern again with my eyes closed. One cycle later I could see the flash of lightning beyond my closed eyelids. Be still and let your light shine. I told myself. I stood and let my eyes flutter open. The whiteness of the clouds was now a deep gray with a spider web of lightning flashes. The lines of light froze in the sky then slowly faded away after a few seconds. I had never seen lightning like this. Around the lightning another shape formed a person. This time the lightning filled the man with color as he approached.

It clicked who he was as I ran toward him and threw myself in his arms, "Papa!"

"Arielle," he said, squeezing me.

"You're real. I can feel you." I became emotional and let the tears escape.

He wiped them away with his thumbs cupping my face. "Don't be sad."

"I'm happy to see you. Wait, am I dead?"

He chuckled and released me, "No, it isn't your time. This is an amazing gift that Madame Brulé has, isn't it?"

"You feel so real, but like a dream."

"Yes, it does. She can help you find your way, by giving you this ability to submerge into your subconscious completely. Next time start with a prayer for guidance just like you used to."

"Okay Papa, I will."

"You have all the answers you need inside of you. God will provide them to you. I'm proud of you, you are learning to be still."

"I'm trying. I know I have fallen away and figured I could do this all on my own. Now I know I can't."

"I had many friends I relied on. Next time you read my book that I left for you, a new chapter will be revealed to you about Madame Brulé now that you have met her."

"How can you write in a book if you are dead?" I asked, frankly.

"It's already there, but you weren't ready to experience it. Continue to ground yourself and listen to everything around you. It will help you grow and learn more."

"I think I understand."

"You will in time. I know you will."

A loud gurgling sound filled my ears like a plug being pulled from a bathtub. Madame Brulé's voice said, "Time's up!"

"Wait, I'm not ready," I cried.

"You can visit another time, I promise," she said, coming into view. The clouds swirled around us creating a wind tunnel that fit in the palm of her hand growing smaller and smaller as the kitchen reformed around us. We sat at the small table with our teacups still steaming. Closing her palm, she snapped her fingers once and glitter sprinkled from the ceiling, disappearing before it reached the floor.

I sat there watching her sip her tea and place it back on the saucer. "I think we are going to be good friends," she said.

"I sure hope so. That was amazing."

"I'm glad you liked it and I hope that you found some peace and direction."

"Yes, it was a good start. Thank you."

"You're welcome. Drink up." She motioned with her hand for me to have some tea. "Your Mother will be looking for you soon."

Just then Mama came into the kitchen. "I was wondering what happened to you," she said.

"Madame Brulé invited me for some tea," I told her.

"Did you tell her that we will be back here with you in less than a year's time?" Mama asked, giving Madame a wink and a smile with her shoulders shrugged almost touching her ears.

I blushed. "No, I didn't mention that yet."

Madame Brulé cupped her mouth, "I'd be honored to help you with your special day. Do you have a date yet?"

"No, we are still exploring that part."

"Well, let me know as soon as you have a date."

"We do have a venue," I offered. "We are having it at River Road Plantation."

Her thin eyebrows raised as her full lips turned up, "That'll be lovely. You'll have a *full* attendance," she said emphasizing the word full.

I glanced at Mama to see if she was following the conversation.

"Dixie is finishing up with the alterations and I think we're going to grab a bite to eat if you are done with your tea," Mama said, motioning with her hand it was time to follow her even if I wasn't finished yet.

212

I looked down at my tea that was barely touched just as Madame Brulé spoke. "It was lovely chatting with you, and we should do this again sometime," she said, picking up my cup.

I rose and walked toward Mama as she cupped my face. "You are going to make such a beautiful bride. I can't wait to pick out your dress."

"Thank you, Mama." I turned to look at Madame Brulé and with a nod said, "Thank you again."

Mama was all smiles as she waved to Madame, "Bye."

We walked down St. Charles Avenue to the streetcar and hopped on heading toward Lee Circle. The streetcar rounded the circle and continued onto Carondelet Street making the last stop at Gravier Street. Dixie and I bounced off the streetcar waiting for our moms to join us.

I locked arms with Dixie and whispered to her, "You are going to make a stunning bride. I am so excited for you and Ernie and the little one on the way."

She giggled, "Thank you, I can't believe this is really happening. And to think I almost tossed this life away."

"Funny how you never know what path you will take," I reflected.

Letting her arm go we stepped into the crisscrossed red brick courtyard walking toward a dark brown awning with white letters that read 'The Windsong Court Hotel'. I opened the golden front door letting Dixie lead our group inside. Dixie and her mom sat on the plush couch around the rectangle coffee table. Mama and I both sat on either side in the overstuffed armchairs. The coffee table was set with delicate China with small strawberry patterns. We each settled on our selections of tea, assortment of sweets and sandwiches.

"I can't remember the last time I was here," Mama said.

Mrs. DeeDee remarked, "Me either. This'll be a nice treat to celebrate our bride to be."

Dixie smiled, "Thank you mom, I'm really enjoying this day with everyone."

The food and laughter made it an afternoon to remember.

In a blink of an eye, it was the wedding day for Dixie and Ernie. Everyone was in place at the Degauss House waiting for the bride to present herself. I looked out into the sea of people ready to stand from their white chairs. Charlie caught my eye and I smiled at him as my mind wandered to what our wedding would be like.

The sounds of violins playing Pachelbel's Canon in D filled the courtyard as Dixie stepped into view. Everyone in unison stood and turned to watch her glide down the aisle holding her father's arm. I took the time to fluff my dark green satin dress and check my mile-high puffed sleeves before Dixie made her way down the aisle. I positioned my own bouquet to be ready for the hand off of her peach rose bouquet filled with white baby's breath and green filler. Her wedding was flawless. The reception transitioned into the evening filled with dancing, drinking and laughter.

In Charlie's arms I asked him as we slowly danced, "Are you ready for all this?"

"If this's what I have to do to spend the rest of my life with you, absolutely."

"I'm ready. I know Mama has given us her blessing. When can we pick a date?"

Charlie led me into a twirl and scooped me back into his arms, "I'm waiting on you," he said with a smirk.

"Me?" I said a little too loud.

"Yes, you."

"What about during carnival? Most people won't be working that week."

"Whatever you want," Charlie said.

"I'm totally going to start planning this tonight!" I warned him.

"I'm ready."

"But where are we going to live? What about your alligator farm?"

"Arielle, let me worry about that stuff you just plan this wedding. Okay?"

"I'll try to stay out of it, but you know I can't help myself."

The song ended and Charlie gave me a little dip and escorted me off the dance floor.

CHAPTER TWENTY-THREE

My Turn

My head was swirling with what to do first. I thought to myself I had the location picked out and now the date of February 8, 1986. Ms. LuLu surely would do the catering. I knew where to get my dress. Who should I ask to be my bridesmaids other than Dixie? I wondered. I should ask Charlie how many groomsmen that would help me decide. Oh, and invitations don't forget about those!

Mama and I were at House of Brulé once again for my last dress fitting. Madame Brulé greeted us by opening the front door before we were even on the steps. "Welcome! Are we excited?" She waved to us to come up.

"Yes, Ma'am! I'm so ready," I beamed at her.

"Thank you for the invitation. I wouldn't miss this for the world. I'm looking forward to seeing the plantation again, it has been quite a while."

After a perfect fitting Madame Brulé zipped the dress away in the white bag handing the precious cargo to me with both arms, "Thank you for everything," I smiled.

"My pleasure."

"I guess that is the last thing to do," Mama said.

"Yes, that is it."

"Let's go home, one last time," Mama said to me as we walked down the sidewalk toward home.

"Oh, Mama, don't do that!"

"Well, this is the last night I will have my baby girl at home. The house's going to be so quiet."

"But Aunt Mabel and all the cousins are staying at the house for the week, that'll help," I offered up.

"True," she said solemnly.

Clutching the dress, I leaned over and gave her a kiss on the cheek when we paused to cross the street. "I love you Mama."

"I love you too sweetie."

The house was bustling with family when we got home. It was nice having a full house like we used to when Papa was still alive. The long dinner table was being used again. I watched the twinkle in Mama's eyes from all the activity. I wondered if this will be the spark she needs to start fostering again.

"A toast to the bride and her lovely mother!" Aunt Mabel raised her wine glass high above her head, "To many years of new life for you both."

"Cheers!" Everyone clinked their glasses and the chatter continued. In time, one by one, each person faded back to their rooms for the evening.

Mama and I sat in the kitchen as she reached for my hand. "I am very proud of you Arielle, and I know Papa is too."

"Thank you, Mama."

"Go get some sleep, you have a big day tomorrow."

"I'm tired."

"The hairdresser will be here at 9 am," she reminded me.

"Okay, goodnight. I love you Mama."

"Love you more."

I traced my finger up the banister trying to take in all the memories of the house, good and bad. I placed Papa's book on my lap once I was settled in my bed. I said to him in my head looking at the closed book, *I wish you were going to be here tomorrow. Like, for real!* Hugging the book, I put it on my bedside table and pulled the covers up to my neck. I prayed, *Dear God, please keep me safe and grant me a good night's sleep. Bless all our families who have come to be with us. Be with me tomorrow as I get married to Charlie. Amen.*

My eyes fluttered open from the sounds of a light knocking. "Arielle? You need to get up," Mama said as she opened my door and went straight to the window to open it. The sunlight poured in and little dust particles danced in the breeze she created from moving the drapes.

I stayed in bed and gave a huge stretch under the covers. Mama tugged them off me and patted my exposed belly. "Eek, your hands are cold Mama!" I said pushing them away.

"You need to get moving, the hairdresser will be here in an hour," she said, leaving the room and closing the door.

I pulled the covers back up to my neck and thought to myself, Today is the day. I smiled thinking about Charlie.

The morning flew by, everyone had left to head to the plantation leaving just Mama and I in the house. She tucked a piece of my hair back into place and smiled looking over my white dress. "This turned out to be a stunning dress on you. I love the lace at the top and the satin at the bottom, but it is a little low cut in the front," she commented.

"Mama, that isn't helpful now."

"I'm sorry," she said, shaking her head, "But the bow in the back is super cute."

"And that is the part I wanted to take off." I laughed at our different tastes.

"Are you ready?" she asked.

"As ready as I am going to be."

"Let's go."

Mama had a white Lincoln Town Car parked out front to drive us to the plantation. "Okay, when we get there I will be dropped off and then your driver will have you come back by yourself so the photographer can get some pictures of you arriving."

The drive seemed to take forever. Once we arrived, things went just as Mama had planned. She waved at me as we pulled away. I watched out the back window as Mama pointed to the photographer and was telling him how to take the pictures. Turning back around I laughed to myself watching her take charge. The Town Car pulled out onto the main road and traveled a bit to turn back toward the plantation.

The driver opened the partition between us a crack. "Are you ready?" he asked.

"Yes, thank you for asking," I said a little hesitantly.

"Here we go," he said with a chuckle.

I peered through the cracked partition and looked out the front of the driver's window. The doors clicked and locked as the Town Car sped forward taking the corner a little too fast. I could see the lined oak trees clipping by us way too fast. "What are you doing?" I yelled at the driver.

"Just having a little fun," he laughed as his hairy hand poked through the dividing window, opening it all the way.

Gasping, I frantically pulled on the door handle, "Mr. Wolf! Let me go!"

"Are you sure you want to get out going this fast?" he continued to poke fun at me. The trees now blurred together due to the speed we were traveling.

"How is any of this possible? There aren't even that many trees" I pointed out.

"You're right," he said and snapped his fingers once. Time froze as we began to levitate. My body rose from the seat as my veil and dress floated round me in the Town Car. We slipped into the next realm as Mr. Wolf's laughter filled my ears.

ABOUT THE AUTHOR

Born in NOLA, but primarily raised in Slidell, Louisiana I love the lure of Voodoo and other haunted folklore of this area. I am a believer in the trinity and evil spirits. I do not practice Voodoo. I am a fiction writer with a flair for the paranormal. My hobbies other than writing include creating art such as pottery, painting, and crafts. I enjoy the beach and an excellent cup of coffee. I am joyfully married and we live with two little fluffy pups and have open our home for children in foster care. As a foster mom I believe God didn't give me my own children so I can help raise other kiddos in their time of need.

Made in USA - North Chelmsford, MA
1308690_9798985844603
03.17.2022 1509